The Bar Z Ranch

The Bar Z Ranch

KAY FARLOW

Noble House
Baltimore, Maryland

The Bar Z Ranch

Library of Congress
Cataloging-in-Publication Data
ISBN 1-56167-767-1

Library of Congress Card Catalog Number:
2002094059

Published by

8019 Belair Road, Suite 10
Baltimore, Maryland 21236

Manufactured in the United States of America

To my grandparents
and the stories they told me about life on the prairie.

CONTENTS

THE BAR Z RANCH
PART TWO

FOREWORD

It all started on a farm near Springfield, Illinois where Zach was born in June, 1848, an only child. In 1849, Zach's father went to California, for the Gold Rush. He thought he would get rich. In a few months, he took the fever and died. He was buried in Sacramento, California by the Mason Lodge. His mother tried to keep the farm going, but it was very hard. She later remarried and her new husband took over the running the farm.

Both Zach and his stepfather worked hard on the farm day after day. When the Civil War came along in the 1860s, the neighbors felt Zach and his stepfather would do more for the war effort by producing much needed food.

The hard work took its toll, but they kept the farm going. During the war he tried to enlist, but he was too young. He then enlisted as an Indian Scout under General Sheridan and served two years in late 1860s and early 1870s in Kansas and Oklahoma. He would come home on leave once in a while

In his early 20s, he met the girl that would be his partner for life. Mandy was only sixteen when she came from Ohio to stay the summer with her uncle. She was one of six girls and one boy. Finding a husband and new home was the only thing she could think about. She loved the beautiful county and would take long walks along the tree shaded road near her uncle's farm. On one of these walks, she met Zach as he was riding his horse on the way to his friend's farm nearby. As he rode on down the road, she made up her mind he was the man for her.

Over the next few weeks, Zach called on Mandy many times. By the end of the summer, he asked her to be his wife. In the years to follow, they had two sons and four daughters.

She was so happy and enjoyed living and caring for her big beautiful home. Disappointment came to her beautiful dreams when Zach decided to go again with General Sheridan for a short time. He came home on leave every once in a while.

This is their story.

THE BAR Z RANCH
PART ONE

CHARACTERS

Zachary Denson — Zach
Almeda Denson — Mandy
Mark & Forrest — Their Sons
Bess, Mary, Gracie, & Lucy—Their daughters
Bob & Ruth Morgan) — Neighbors in Springfield
Will — Captain of the Wagon Train
Bob Allen — Owner of the Store in Chivington
Bill & Helen Williams — Friends in Chivington
Little Bill, George, & Cathy — Children of Bill and Helen
Howard & Betty Johnson — Well Digger and his wife
Joe — Bill's Foreman
Lumberman — Worked in Lamar
Miss Snyder — School Teacher
Mr. Crocker — Owner of the Bank
Mike Wallace — Sheriff
Hank — One of Bill's Hired Hands
Jim Reaves — Young Stranger
Ben Conover — Dr. Ben, the Town Doctor
Alice Conover — Doctor's Wife
Ezra Cooper— Coop, owner of newspaper
Angel — The Williams' Dog
George Fleming
Nancy—Wife of George
Mack— First husband of Bess
Wes— Second husband of Bess, First husband of Lucy
Charles— Husband of Mary

CHAPTER ONE

MOVING WEST

The time was winter early 1870s, the war had been over a few years. A young man stood by the fence looking over the fields of stubble left by the corn crop. Zach was his name, and he was handsome and six feet tall with dark hair and a mustache. His eyes were so blue, like deep pools of water, they held your gaze for just a moment. A breeze was blowing the little bit of snow left on the ground. As the snow moved around it would stick to the corn stocks left on the ground. It was cold, very cold, and the snow felt like ice pellets hitting his face. As he set on a stump left by a tree blown down in the last big wind, he was deep in thought. He had just received another letter from his friend in Colorado. What was he to do? He wanted so much to give up the farm and go west to be with his friend. It seemed every year the wind storms got worse. Would they blow the house or barn down next time? As he read the letter again he decided that was what he wanted to do, move to Colorado and own a nice ranch with cattle and the freedom of the open spaces.

As he walked slowly back to the warmth of the barn, he thought of his lovely wife. She was so young and beautiful with her soft reddish blonde hair; she was so tiny, just five foot tall. She always had a smile for him when he came into the house. He loved her so much and wanted the very best for her and their two little boys. Mark, just four years old, was a normal child with all of the ambitions little boys have. Forrest, just turned two, was still their baby. Everyone called him "Baby."

What would Mandy say? She loved this place and having her friends around her. How was he going to get the money to make the move? He would have to sell his farm, but that was another hard decision as this farm was handed down from his father. He remembered reading the paper a few weeks back, Horace Greeley had said "Go West, Young Man, Go West." He would have to talk to Mandy and convince her that he wanted to make the move, and life would be good on the range. She loved their friends that had moved to Colorado. He hoped she would want to make the move to be with them.

Zach finished up the chores in the barn and pulling his coat tight around him, he headed for the house. When he came in Mandy said, "Where have you been? Supper has been ready for a long time."

Zach gathered her in his arms, holding her close and stroking her hair gently, "Mandy my dear, I want to talk to you about moving out to Colorado. As you know Bill and Helen have been asking us to come to them and this last letter really moved me. I know you will like it out there in the wide open spaces, lots of land and a chance to make a good living for us and the boys. We've had some bad storms lately and I am afraid that someday they'll blow down the house or the barn. I've been worried and I think this move is for the best."

"Move so far away, leave all of our friends, and how can we take all of our beautiful things way out there?"

"We won't be going right away. First, I must sell the farm so that we'll have the money to live on until we can start making a profit from the cattle."

As Mandy cleaned up the supper dishes, she was doing a lot of thinking about the move to Colorado. She loved her husband so much and wanted to do what he wanted. The thought of moving so far away scared her but knowing that Zach would always be by her side to protect and take care of her and the boys gave her comfort.

They talked way into the night about the move and as Mandy drifted off to sleep, she decided that she wouldn't give him any more objection.

The next morning Zach rode over to talk with neighbor Bob

Morgan. Bob had wanted to buy his farm for some time, but Zach always said that he didn't want to sell. Now his mind was made up. He was going to ask him if he still wanted to buy. Bob's place was next to his and by buying his farm it would make Bob's one of the largest in the country.

Bob was happy to make the deal with Zach, and they talked for a long time before reaching a price they both agreed on. At last everything was in order and both men rode into Springfield, Illinois to file the necessary papers.

As the men rode back Zach said, "We don't want to start on our trip for two or three months if that's all right with you. You can start working the land any time as of now it's yours." Bob said it would be fine for them to stay in the house until the weather was more settled.

Zach hurried home to tell Mandy of the sale and it would be a few months before the big move. He had to write to Bill and Helen informing them they were coming.

He was a happy man as he made his way home to tell Mandy about his deal with Bob and of his plans for their future.

Mandy met him at the door, "Well how did it go? Is Bob going to buy our farm?"

Zach answered her after he took off his coat and stood by the fire as it was still very cold outside. "I have it all worked out, we'll take all of the things we'll need to get started. While I was in town I inquired about a wagon and oxen for us to make the trip and also about the freight wagons that haul for the people that can't take everything with them. I trust these fellows, they'll start when I send the word."

Mandy's friends heard they had sold the farm and about them moving to Colorado. They came over to see her and hear the details of the trip west.

Mandy said, "Oh, I don't want to leave all of you. I'll be so lonesome in that desolated place. I hear you don't have neighbors for miles and miles."

They tried to comfort her. Ruth said, "You'll make new friends. You're such a nice person and we're sure they will have a church in a nearby town. Be sure you make time for church, and the boys will be a comfort for you and keep you busy."

Zach and Mandy made their plans to make the move in early spring so they could be settled before winter came. Zach bought a big wagon and four oxen. Packing the wagon was a big job with all of the dishes, pots, pans, eating utensils and all the food needed for the long trip. At least 100 lbs. of flour and 100 lbs. of sugar. They had to have dried beef, cured ham, 100 lbs. of dried beans, dried fruit and all the things she had canned. Bedding was needed for sleeping and keeping warm if the nights turned cold. It took a lot of clothes for the boys and themselves.

The children were not sure of what was going on with all of the packing. Mark asked his mother, "What are you doing with all of our stuff? Here is my wagon and our toys, we want them in the wagon with the other things."

Mandy answered him, "Don't worry, we'll put your wagon in the big one with our furniture. Now Mark, let me explain to you what is going on. Papa wants us to move to a new land way out west. There will be lots of space for you to play, and we'll have cows, chickens, and all kinds of things you like." As Mandy continued with her packing, she thought to herself, "Oh, I forgot the coffee and tea. We must have them. I just know I've forgotten something, what could it be?

Mandy wrapped her prize glasses and other wedding gifts.

There were vases, plates and all those breakable things that required a lot of protection for the long trip. "Oh, there's my music box." She held it in her hands, looking at it for a long time and holding it to her heart "I hope we're doing the right thing. Zach loved me so much, he gave this to me when we were married. I'll have it always by my side. I'm going to take this in our wagon."

Someone came to the door. She opened it and there were her good friends. Ruth said, "We've something for your trip. We made you three sunbonnets to wear, the sun is hot on the prairies, you'll need them to protect you from the sun. Your husband and the boys had better get some big brimmed hats to protect them also."

Mandy made tea and brought it to them. "I'm sorry for the old cups. All of my good things are packed."

Mandy started to cry. "I guess I'll have to get used to this for a while."

"Please don't cry, everything will be all right. Now, we must leave, and let you get to your packing."

"I'm almost done, if I leave anything be sure to check the house and take anything that I might have left. I would want you to have it."

It was a nice warm spring day the first week of April. The men from the freight line left the big wagons with Zach for loading. Bob came over to help load as it was too big of a job for one man. Trunks were filled with quilts, all made tenderly by hand, and doilies and pillow cases. There were enough chairs, tables, and bedroom furniture for the whole house. Next went the barrels of dishes and all the other breakables. The freight wagons were now finished. Their wagon was to be loaded next, with the things they would need for the trip. The final touch, wash tubs and water barrels were tied to the sides of the wagon.

Neighbors came from far and near to bid them good-bye. The yard was filled with buggies, wagons, and horses. Zach had lived in this house all of his life and had many friends.

Mandy said to the boys, "Now into the wagon with you, the mattress will be soft to ride on."

With the boys in the wagon Mandy went to each of the women giving them a hug, "Good-bye my friends, it'll be all right. I'll write to you all about our adventures."

Bob Morgan said, "I know you'll do well, you are a young man with a beautiful young wife."

By mid morning the family was on the way to their great adventure. They headed south from Springfield to East St. Louis. The roads were good and all went well for them. Each night they would stop and make camp because it was impossible to travel the roads at night. Mandy had things prepared to make it easy to fix the evening meal. Every morning she would make a lunch for them to eat on the road so they wouldn't have to stop at noon. They traveled the one hundred miles in seven days.

Mandy enjoyed the ride down the road. It was so nice to see the green grass and the trees. The flowers along the side of the road smelled so sweet. Across the meadows small creeks were running, making a splashing noise as they ran over a down tree or rocks. The early spring flowers were blooming along the creek bank in an array of colors, red, yellow, blue, and orange. Every once in a while a butterfly would drift by and then a bee would light on one of the flowers bending the stem over to touch the flower next in line.

Mandy was thinking to herself, "All of this beauty and all I have to look forward to is dry grass and sagebrush, wild animals, snakes, and above all, no people to visit and talk with."

Zach said, "What? I didn't hear you. Were you saying something?"

"Oh no, I was just thinking about our new home."

"So was I. I'm sure we'll have a great time on our ranch. The boys will enjoy the great freedom of the range."

Mandy was quiet the rest of the way, "I'll have to make do with my lot." She said under her breath.

They finally arrived in East St. Louis, with people everywhere, the streets were full of wagons, carts, and oxen.

Mandy remarked, "Where are all of these people going?"

"I hope they aren't going the same place we are."

Zach stopped the wagon on the side of the road. He saw some men ahead of them. He walked over to them and asked, "Where can we find out about a boat for crossing the Mississippi?"

"Go down to the river front about a mile. One will leave in a day or so when he has a full load. You had better leave your wagon here, there are too many wagons on the road."

Zach came back to the wagon and told Mandy he would have to walk down to the river front to check on a boat.

"Mandy, I want you and the boys to be safe while I'm gone. You take this gun and hold it on your lap and use it if necessary."

"I can't use a gun. I don't know anything about guns!"

"You have to protect our things. Thieves are everywhere, especially in the city. They steal wagons and sell them to others for money. I'll be back as soon as I can get passage on a boat."

Zach hurried down the road and was soon out of sight.

Mandy and the boys waited for a long time or at least it seemed to be a long time. Mandy said, "He has been gone so long. Where can he be?"

Mandy was beginning to get worried, "It's getting dark, and we haven't had supper yet. What if he's gone all night?"

Just then Zach walked around the corner of the wagon and

heard her, "I wouldn't leave you alone all night."

Mandy jumped down from the wagon and gave him a big hug, "We're so glad to have you back."

"We'll set up camp over there in the trees. I talked with the owner and he said it would be all right."

Zach unhitched the oxen, and Mandy set about preparing their supper. "Mark, help your Papa gather some wood for the fire."

It wasn't long before things were cooking. After they had their meal, Zach said, "I have a surprise for all of you. Here are some sweets for the boys and for you my dear, little cakes. I got them from a baker shop in town. You have to see that place. Shops of all kinds, meat shop, bakery, and general stores, such fun. I also asked the owner of this place to watch our wagon. Tomorrow we'll go into town, how do you like that boys?"

"Oh! How nice it'll be, and the boys will have a good time seeing something different. They've never been in a big town before." Mandy was real excited about the day to come.

Zach and Mandy with the boys walked into town the next morning. Mandy had never been in a big city and was thrilled with all of the stores. So many beautiful things to buy, but she decided that she didn't need them or could use them where she was going.

While they were in town they found out that the flat bed boat would be leaving in two days.

So before the sun was up the second day they were on the way to the dock where the boat was tied. The traffic was heavy, but everyone was going the same way.

Mandy remarked, "Will there be room for all of these wagons on the boat? What if we get on the wrong boat?"

"Don't worry, there are several boats going to different places. I've got the papers with the name of the boat and a receipt for the money I paid him, it'll be all right."

Zach pulled the wagon into the line waiting to board.

It seemed to take a long time before they got close to their boat. The wagons moved slowly along the dock. Each wagon driver selected the boat he was to be on. At last their turn came. Getting on the boat proved to be difficult. The oxen objected to the ramp. The men loading the wagons had to take hold of the reins of the lead oxen and pull them aboard.

CHAPTER TWO

UP THE RIVERS

After a time, the wagons were settled on the boat, the oxen were tied and the wagons wheels blocked. It was necessary for the wagons to be secure as they might roll off the open end of the flat bed boat. With everything taken care of Zach, Mandy, and the boys went to the upper deck to enjoy the short trip across the Mississippi River.

Mark said, "Oh boy, this is great! A ride on a real boat, I've never even seen a boat, and now we get to ride on one!"

Zach answered, "You just wait until you see the other one. A big steamer will take us up the Missouri River. We'll be on it for several days, sleep in cabins and eat in a large room in the center of the boat. During the day time we'll walk along the railings, watch the water and all of the things along the shore. We might see some animals drinking from the banks of the river."

"Won't it be fun to just relax and let the Captain do all of the work?" Mandy said with a smile.

The short trip across the Mississippi River was uneventful. While crossing the river, Zach talked with the Captain and asked him which steamer he recommended for the trip up the Missouri. He suggested that they try to get accommodations on the *Robert Bell*, as it was one of the best.

The Captain docked the boat on the other side of the river in St. Louis, Missouri. The wagons were taken off the boat slowly, one at a time. At last it was their turn. Moving the oxen was a slow process. Finally, they were on the way up the street. A lot was set aside for the wagons until the passage on the steamer could be arranged. A guard was posted to see that no one would bother the wagons and oxen.

After everything was settled and the oxen fed, Zach said, "Let's go into town, I think we'd better pick up some additional things we might need. I talked to some of the men on the boat and they said we would need more rope, an ax, and some buckets of grease for the wagon wheels. We should get some more flour if we can fit it in. Also, we should have replacements for a broken harness, just in case. I have only one rifle and one hand gun. I think I'll get two more, as the ones we have could get lost or broken."

"More guns! I'm feeling more scared all of the time."

Zach held her in his arms, "There, none of this. We'll need the guns to hunt for meat. Come on, boys, let's go to town and see what they have there."

They walked into town enjoying the sights of the stores, hotels, and restaurants. Zach said, "Let's have lunch in the restaurant. You won't have to work all day."

Mark exclaimed, "Oh goody, I've never eaten in a real restaurant."

After buying their supplies and arranging to have a man take them back to the wagon, they looked for the office of the steamer company. The deposit for the trip on the *Robert Bell* was made. Zach felt they were lucky to find the space available for the trip up the river. The Captain said the ship would sail by the end of the week. While they were in the office, they met the Wagon Master of a wagon train that would be traveling on the same trail Zach had planned.

Zach hadn't thought about a wagon train but the Wagon Master explained that it would be much better to travel in groups to help each other and for the company. Mandy, Zach, and the boys made their way back to the lot where they left the wagon. Their things had been delivered, and they soon had everything put away. It was time for the boys to go to bed. Mandy visited with the women of the other wagons. They all enjoyed telling about where they were from, comparing recipes, talking about their children, and most of all their husbands.

Zach and the other men went off to the other side of the lot to talk about things men talk about. Many topics were covered. The work that had to be done on the trail and their plans for the new homes they expected to build.

The wagons were in camp for two days. On Saturday, Zach's wagon was the first in the line to board the steamer. It was the third day of May, a beautiful spring day with the sun rising over the water of the big Mississippi River. The water in the river moved slow and lazily from shore to shore. Looking at the water made a person feel sort of slow and lazy. A few boats were on the river, even at this early hour. Some were small fishing boats and others were flat bed boats carrying people from one side of the river to the other. Because the ship was so large they had very little trouble with the oxen boarding. It took a while to get all of the wagons settled at one end of the ship and the oxen tied at the other. As they were going to be on the ship several days plans had to be made to feed and water the animals.

The boilers were fired up, and they began to move up river toward the mouth of the Missouri. With a full load the ship set out for the middle of the Mississippi River and turned its bow upstream. The ship, *The Robert Bell*, did well in the slow moving river. As they reached the mouth of the Missouri, the Captain found it was difficult to enter the river because of the fast water flowing down stream.

They found a lot of mud and debris in the water. The Captain had to let the ship slip backward into the Mississippi. He ordered a major head of steam and tried again and again, but he was only able to get six knots forward while the river was flowing four knots in the opposite direction. With a great burst of steam, he moved the ship to the northern bank of the Missouri and caught a reverse current which helped him enter the main channel. Another burst of speed brought the ship into calmer water. Just as darkness fell, the Captain pushed ahead to safe water.

Traveling up the Missouri River was an adventure. The river was known as The Big Muddy, the longest river in America. Sandbars and jagged tree trunks hung over the river. When the trees leaned over into the water, you could hear the limbs rubbing against the boat. A tree could rip the bottom out of the boat.

The Captain and his men had to keep a close watch. He didn't want to lose his cargo, animals, or his passengers. Time went by. Everyone was helping watch for the tree limbs. The Captain said, "Thanks for all of your help. We'll have to continue the watch all the way because it doesn't get any better as we make our way upstream."

Watching the water and trees was exciting for the boys. They would squeal each time a limb would come close by.

Mark yelled, "Look, Papa, another one coming. Watch it go by."

Zach and the boys leaned over the railing and watched the water for a long time. "Look, boys, over there. Is that a deer? I think it is. Isn't he pretty? Look at those big brown eyes. I'm sure he sees you, wave to him."

Mark answered, "Papa, the deer can't wave to us!"

Mandy was busy with the women, making their plans for the rest of the trip. She suggested some games for the children to play while on board to help them pass the time.

On the fourth day, May seventh, they reached the city of Boonville. "Here we'll dock a few days and let the animals off to roam about and get some exercise. From now on, it'll be a long trip for them," the Captain explained to the passengers.

Boonville was a turning point for several trails. Caravans set forth for the Santa Fe Trail, Yellowstone, and the distant forts beyond the head of the Missouri River.

Zach suggested, "Let's look around the town and see what they have here. The Captain said there is another town up the road a ways called Franklin. Do you feel like a walk to look at the new town?"

The boys were glad to be able to run around a little.

"I would like to take a walk. Being on the ship makes a person feel the need for some solid ground. Why are there two towns so close together?" Mandy asked.

Zach told her the reason for forming the other town. He said that the town of Boonville was flooded so many times the people owning the buildings near the river decided that they wanted to build on higher ground. They were tired of being flooded out each year.

Franklin was a beautiful town of about six thousand with a

newspaper, lawyers, good schools, and a lively concern for all that was happening in the west.

Zach said, "I think I'll pick up a newspaper to see what's going on." He found a paper stand on the side of the street.

"No news of back home. It's all about the west, ships, and local things."

On May twelfth, the steamer resumed its journey to Blacksnake Hills. In a few days they docked in Independence. The Captain suggested they not go into town. "This is the rowdiest town in the west. I think it's best the women and children stay aboard. You men can go, but I advise against it as you don't know who might attack you for your money or just for fun."

Zach told Mandy, "That's not for me. We'll stay aboard and walk around the deck. We can see the town from here at a safe distance."

They watched the men that worked on the ship take the animals on to the dock to get a little exercise.

Mandy asked the Captain, "Will our oxen be safe ashore?" "My men know how to handle ruffians because they're also rough men. They get good pay for what they do, and they wouldn't want to lose a good job."

While they were docked in Boonville, the Captain found out his favorite store owner had moved to St. Joseph. The trip continued on, but they didn't stop at Blacksnake Hills as they planned but pushed on to Fort Leavenworth for a short stop. Several officers in the cavalry came aboard. They were on their way to St. Joseph to receive new orders.

The boys enjoyed talking with the soldiers, "What is it like to be a soldier? Mark asked. "I would like to have a uniform."

Mandy said, "Now Mark, you know you want to be like your Papa and work the land."

Zach answered, "Mandy don't worry about your son. All boys dream of a uniform at times."

The Captain was glad to be on his way to see his friend in St. Joseph. This would be the end of the trip for him, and he was in a hurry to get back to St. Louis and pick up more eager passengers for their trip upriver and on to the west.

Zach said, "My dear, we are on our way to Colorado." He

assured her all was well. Everything was going as planned.

They arrived in St. Joseph on May twenty-fifth. At this point, they had to leave the ship and transfer to another flat boat to take them across the Missouri River to the Kansas side.

Zach looked down the river toward the dock where the flat bed boats were tied. They looked to be in bad shape, not like those on the Mississippi River. He said to himself, "I hope they'll stay afloat until we reach the other side of the river."

The process of leaving the ship was carried on in an orderly manner with each wagon following the one in front. As the wagons reached the bank of the river, they started down the river road toward the dock where the small boats were ready to receive them. The procession went slowly, and at last they were ready to go on the ferry. The oxen had no trouble in boarding. In a short time, they were on the way to the other side of the Missouri.

After docking, the Wagon Master directed them toward the road they were to take for the first leg of the trip. By noon, the wagon train had assembled on the Kansas side of the river and immediately started on the trail. That afternoon they covered the first six miles of the trip west.

CHAPTER THREE

THE WAGON TRAIN

It didn't take long to cover the first six miles. They made camp by putting all of the wagons in a circle, and the men started several cooking fires. Each of the women brought out the necessary cooking utensils needed to prepare the evening meal.

Six wagons in all made the circle, the Wagon Master's wagon had, in addition to their own supplies, emergency supplies—reins, grease, rope etc, and two large logs the length of the wagon. Four men helped him as drivers and trail riders.

Each man had his job to do and each was experienced in his own field, scouting the trail and others in handling the oxen and the wagons.

Of the five other wagons, one had men going to the Silver Mines west of Denver, Colorado and one was going to Ft. Laramie, Wyoming. Two of the wagons were carrying people to Oregon and Zach's was the last of the six. After the meals were finished and the cooking materials were tucked away everyone sat around the camp fires enjoying conversation with the people in the other wagons.

The Wagon Master spoke to the group, "We must have a meeting. As you know my name is William Morse, as I want to be 'one of you' please call me Will."

Zach answered, "I'm Zachary, but everybody calls me Zach. This is my wife Almeda, and we all call her Mandy. We're glad to have you lead us on this long journey."

The people on the other wagons introduced themselves.

Everyone greeted each other with 'hellos' and handshakes.

Will continued, "Tomorrow will be the start of a long trip. It's about one hundred miles before we reach the Big Blue River. We should try to be there in the next four or five days. This distance can be covered in the allotted time depending on several things, most of all the weather, because if it rains it'll slow us down and breakdowns might happen. We hope this won't occur. Be sure your wheels are well greased and the reins are secure. We don't want to lose any stock or wagons. Each night we'll rest as we have this evening, have a good meal and at that time I'll review the plans for the coming day."

Mandy asked, "When can we find enough water to have a bath, it's been so long and the little boys are so dirty."

Will answered her, "Tomorrow I'm sure we'll run into a little creek. You can plan on that and we can fill our water barrels."

As the camp fires were slowly dying down, everyone prepared for a good night's sleep. Mandy put the boys into the wagon and climbed in herself.

"It's going to be a little tight with all the things we have in the wagon."

Zach said, "I'll sleep on the ground so you and the boys will have more room. Give me a blanket, I can make a good bed right here under the wagon."

By the time the sun was up the next morning, Will was shouting, "Everybody up! Let's have a quick breakfast and we'll be on our way."

It was smooth going and no stops, across fields and meadows covered with grass and brightly colored flowers. In the beginning of the trip the travelers could see a few trees. This part of Kansas was lightly forested and had a rich alluvial loam soil. With the adequate rainfall the grass and flowers grew abundantly. At times they came upon unbroken ground with rocks and ruts around each turn. In the meadows the dew could cling to the boots of the men and women walking beside the wagons. Later in the day the dew would give way to dust on the trail.

Will came back from scouting the area ahead and said, "Good news, we've found the creek I mentioned in our meeting last night. We'll not stop for our midday meal as it's only about four hours to water and we can make camp for the night."

About 5:00 they saw the trees lining the bank of the creek. All along the train you could hear the people yelling, "Oh boy, water, lots of water, we'll have a good time tonight swimming in the creek."

The wagons were circled again as before. The men and the children gathered wood from the bank of the creek. The fires were started and as soon as they were hot the women had things ready to cook the evening meal. Not having stopped for lunch, all the children were hungry.

Mark said, "I can't wait to eat. Can I have a bite now?"

Mandy answered, "Just you wait for the rest of the meal. It won't be long."

Having enjoyed a good meal, everyone was glad to relax around the fire.

Mandy called to Zach, "Papa, get some buckets of water. I'll put on the fire to warm."

"Right away, I know you and the boys are ready for a nice bath."

Mandy put some of the water in large pans on the fire to heat, and the rest went into the wash tubs. Each boy was popped in a tub and scrubbed good and with their night shirts on they hopped into their bed. After their bath, they felt so good they went to sleep immediately. Mandy took a big pan of warm water into the wagon.

Mandy said, "Papa, I'm going to change all my clothes and have a good wash."

"Give me a towel and some soap, I'll go down to the creek and wash with the rest of the men."

"Don't lose the soap!"

"Don't worry," Zach yelled back to her.

As Mandy went off to sleep she could hear the men yelling and splashing in the creek. She smiled to herself, "Just a bunch of boys."

The next morning everyone was up, feeling so refreshed from their baths and a good night's sleep. They made twenty miles the next day. The next four days were all as good as the first and they were on the schedule Will had planned. The country was so beautiful, everyone enjoyed the trip and were looking forward to the Big Blue River.

Will said to them, "You are doing so well, tomorrow we should reach the river."

When they saw the river the men were worried about the crossing, it looked so wide and deep.

Zach said, "How are we going to cross that?"

Will answered, "Don't worry. I'm prepared."

He pulled the logs out of his wagon, "Here, put these on each side of your wagon and secure them with these ropes. You'll float like a boat."

As they headed for the river, Mandy exclaimed, "Oh I know we'll all be drowned."

"Don't worry. Will knows what he's doing. He has done it many times before."

The men dismounted and pushed the wagons from behind while one of them held the reins. The women and children remained in the wagons, clinging atop their things so they wouldn't get their feet wet. The oxen were lured into the water. Slowly the wagons sank, until it looked as if they must go under. But at the calculated depth they floated. Only a little of the floor got wet. Will had told them to put the flour, sugar and bedding up high so they wouldn't get wet.

The oxen were fine as long as they could feel the bottom, but they got a little scared when they had to swim. The men swam along with them and kept them going. Finally the oxen could feel the bottom again and all went well as they climbed to the other shore.

One by one the wagons were led across the river. Each one having the same experience of floating part way and then reaching the bank on the other side. At last all the wagons made it across.

Will said, "We'll make camp here tonight and get everything back in it's proper place. Tomorrow we'll travel ten more miles to the Little Blue river, it's a lot smaller so you'll find a much smoother crossing."

Each night Mandy found cooking the meals became easier.

As soon as the wagons were in place she would get the iron grate ready to place on the rocks around the fire. It was the nearest thing to a stove top.

She had an iron dutch oven with a lid to bake the biscuits. The bread board was dusted with flour. A little of the sour dough starter was taken from the crock and enough flour added to make biscuits for the evening meal and a little extra for breakfast. A little grease was added to the pot so the biscuits would not stick.

As soon as the water boiled she added the beans that had been soaking since the last stop. The soaking made them soft so they cooked in a short time. Adding a jar of tomatoes she had canned in the fall and a few onions, sometimes a slice of ham, made a good meal. When everything was cooking she placed the frying pan on the hot part of the grate and fried some bacon. Mandy always saved the drippings from the bacon. Of course, the coffee pot was a must.

When the meal was finished Zach would stand the grate on edge to cool. Breakfast would be cooked on the rocks because they couldn't heat the iron grate as it would be to hot to store in the wagon the next morning.

Mandy would change the menus from time to time. Sometimes it would be boiled potatoes and a jar of green beans she had canned the previous year. She was glad they had packed all the canned things because beans and bacon would get tiresome after a while.

They found no problems with the other rivers as they now knew the crossings would work. Many more rivers and many more crossings were yet to come. Thirty five miles to the crossing of the Republican River. On forty miles to cross the Solomon River. South again, following the Smoky Hill River to Great Bend, a long sixty miles. Just before they got to Great Bend they joined the Santa Fe Trail. The trail had been used so much it was like a road, this made traveling much easier.

When they reached Great Bend, Will said, "We'll layover a day to rest before we start on the next forty miles to Fort Laramie."

The Arkansas River was the next to be crossed. It was a big river but it was much easier because it was shallow. The Arkansas River had to be crossed twice, once just after leaving Great Bend and again further up stream toward Fort Laramie. Forty more miles and they would be in Dodge City, Kansas. Dodge City was one of the wildest cities in America, saloons, dance halls, hotels and several general stores. It was the railroad center for the Santa Fe Railroad with repair shops and housing for the men that worked on the line for many miles around.

Everyone on the wagon train was happy to be in the big city, enjoying the sights and doing some shopping for supplies. Will said, "We'll find a good camp sight and stay here for a few days."

Zach, Mandy, and the boys made their way into town. People were everywhere, on horses, in wagons and some walking. Mandy remarked, "This is quite a town. I've never seen so many people with nothing to do but run around and getting themselves into trouble."

"Don't worry, they won't bother us. We'll just go about our own business," Zach advised.

The new supplies were loaded in the wagon and Zach and Mandy settled in for a few days of rest before starting on the last leg of their trip. Early in the morning of the third day the wagon train was on the trail headed west. When they left Dodge City they took the Mountain Branch of the Santa Fe Trail.

Everyone knew this was going to be a long hot trip. It was about one hundred miles to Lamar, Colorado. A dusty hot time was expected as west of Dodge City and on until the foothills of the mountains, only a few trees could be found. The soil was sandy and with little rainfall, mostly in the early spring. By the first of June and on through the summer it was very dry and dusty. Water holes were dry and the rivers ran low.

After a full day on the trail Mandy remarked, "Will this heat and dust ever end?"

"It'll be a least three or four more days and we have to be careful of our water. We aren't sure when we'll reach the next water hole. When we get to Lamar, it'll be only twenty miles to our old friends in Chivington."

Five days on the trail, camping each night and resting for the next day's journey. It was easier to rest and sleep as the nights were cooler than the days. The six wagons of the train made their way down the trail following close to the Arkansas River. At times it was only a trickle, with sandbars between the bank and the water. Some of the sandbars were of quicksand and couldn't be crossed. It was hard to see the water and not be able to reach it.

The wagons had been on the trail for forty-five days and had covered five hundred and ninety miles since they left St. Joseph. Even with the hardships of the long and hard trip it was considered a successful adventure.

Will said, "A very good trip, good times and above all no accidents."

The people of the wagon train paid the balance due Will for his service. Everybody was ready to leave Lamar, Colorado, each one to their own destination. The one wagon with just the men went to the silver mines west of Denver. Heading northwest were the two wagons for Oregon and the one going to Ft. Laramie. Zach and Mandy were to head due north to Chivington. Everybody was saying their good-byes, the men shaking hands all around and the women hugging each other.

Zach reminded his wife, "My dear, it's only twenty miles to Chivington."

Zach and Mandy and their two little boys were on their way, the last twenty miles of a very long trip. They followed the Big Sandy River all the way into Chivington, Colorado.

Zach stopped the wagon a few miles outside of town so that they could arrive in Chivington during the light of day.

CHAPTER FOUR

FINDING THE BW RANCH

Zach and Mandy drove down the road to Chivington. Around noon, on a beautiful day in early July, 1870, they arrived in the small town in southeastern Colorado. They were happy to see this lovely little place. One main street, but everything was there just for the asking. The first thing, the blacksmith's building with a big stable in the back. The fenced yard was big enough to hold several head of horses. The Smithy was out in front of the building and gave them a wave as they passed by.

Several small houses were side by side for a short way and the General Store and Post Office. This was the center of all activity in the small town. The hotel/restaurant was right across the street from the store. White curtains framed the windows, with the sun shining on them they looked like crystal gems. Next door to the hotel were the bank and the Sheriff's office. Further down the street, the saloon and card room. Many horses were tied to the rail in front of the building. All of the saloon business came from the local ranchers, as Chivington was not on the regular trail of the drovers from Texas.

Mandy was excited. With all of the activity when she spotted a little house next door to the General Store. It was the dressmaker's place with lovely dresses and hats showing in the windows. She thought to herself, "They do have pretty things here, maybe the ladies don't always dress in grays and browns. I'll be glad to get rid of these drab things."

As they reached the end of the street a lovely white church

with a bell tower reaching high in the sky. The church was on a small hill and that made the bell tower seem even higher in the sky.

Mandy said, "Oh Papa, this is a wonderful little town. I think I'll like it here."

Zach answered her, "I'm sure we'll find a lot of new friends. Let's turn around and stop at the General Store and ask how to get to Bill's place."

Zach drove the wagon down the street to the store and stopped. He was about to jump down, when a man came out to see them.

Zach asked, "Hi there, do you know the Williams, Bill and his wife Helen? We're their friends from Illinois."

The man was Bob Allen, the store owner, "Yes, Bill said you folks were coming. Follow Rush Creek about two miles west, they are on the right side of the road."

"Thank you, we'll see you again, many times I'm sure."

Zach, Mandy, and the boys enjoyed the ride down the road along the creek. Cottonwood trees grew along the creek banks, making shade for them. On the other side of the road lay the plains of the prairie. The grass covered the ground, here and there a sagebrush and rocks could be seen. Zach thought to himself, "How can anyone raise grain on this barren ground?"

About two miles down the road they saw a ranch house and several out buildings. A big two story house set on the higher ground with a large porch across the front. Three rocking chairs and a small table made it look so inviting. The bunk house located a little way down the rise and it too had a porch with chairs. It looked like a good place for the men that worked on the ranch to relax after a hard day. The ranch looked so successful with the corrals, stable and the horses. At the entrance a big sign, "The BW Ranch."

Before they got to the house, Bill and Helen came running down the road, following close behind, three children, two boys and a beautiful little girl.

"Hi, welcome to Colorado, we're so glad you're here."

Zach called back to them, "We made it! All is well."

He stopped the wagon and Bill reached for Mandy. After helping her down he gave her a big hug. Down came the boys, Mark and Forrest. They were glad to be out of the wagon.

Mark exclaimed, "Come on, Baby, let' run. It's been so long , since we could."

They ran up to the children, "Hi, I'm Mark, and this is Forrest. He isn't very big."

The Williams children all shook hands and the oldest said, "I'm Bill, like my Papa. This is George and my little sister Catherine. We call her Cathy. Come on, we'll show you the barn." George said, "We have a new calf."

Cathy said, "He is such a cute little baby."

As the children ran toward the barn George said, "We've got a bunch of baby chicks also. We can't play with them yet; they are too little. We got new kittens too. It won't be long, when they don't have to be with their mother all of the time, we can play with them too."

When they reached the barn a great big dog came out to meet them. Mark and Forrest were a little afraid of such a big dog and they stopped in their tracks.

Little Bill said, "Don't be scared, she's real nice and won't hurt you a bit."

After a time the boys made friends with the dog and all of the other animals.

Mandy and Helen were hugging each other and holding hands as they walked toward the house.

Bill got into the wagon with Zach, "Go down the road and stop the wagon next to the house. We can unhitch the oxen, take them down to the last shed. I'm sure they would like to have some food and water."

"That'll be fine they've been such good fellows and deserve a good rest."

After the animals were watered and fed the men walked up to the house. Helen had a good dinner all ready and warming on the back of the stove.

Mandy said, "A stove, I've been cooking on camp fire for forty-five days. I'll have to get used to a stove again." The Williams had a big house. Bill had been building on it for several years. Downstairs had two big bedrooms and a large family room that was used for both a dining and a living room. At the far end of the room there was a large fireplace and hearth built of rocks. Helen had a big kitchen with lots of cabinets and a beautiful big stove. Upstairs was just a loft.

Bill said, "Some day we want to divide the loft into two or three bedrooms and make a staircase so it will be easier to get upstairs."

Helen called the children, "It's time to get washed up, and we'll have a nice dinner and talk about our plans."

Bill said, "The children can sleep in the loft, and Zach, you and Mandy can use the other bedroom."

Zach said, "Let's bring in our mattress from the wagon. It will be soft for them to sleep on."

George said, "Goody, we'll have such fun!"

Helen said, "Now you children be good, we'll have a busy day tomorrow."

The children climbed up to the loft. Bill put a gate over the entrance so they wouldn't fall down the ladder. With the children settled, the parents set around the table to make their plans for the next few days.

Zach said, "The first thing I must do is to go to the land office and file my claim for some land."

Bill answered, "I've been looking around for you. I think I've spotted a good place. Let's go and look at it first and if you like it you can make a firm claim, good land is going fast. It's on Rush Creek so water won't be a problem. It'll take a lot of building as there isn't much there but a old sod house."

"Thank you for your help but we don't like to impose on you too long."

Helen said, "It'll be fun having you here."

"As soon as my papers are finalized, we'll start building. Another thing I must do is to transfer my account from Springfield to the local bank."

Bill said, "No problem, I talked with the manager of the bank, and he said he is looking forward to doing business with you."

Mandy asked, "I didn't see a school house when we drove through town. Where do the children go to school?"

Helen answered, "The children are taught by a local woman in her home. When they get to the eighth grade and want to go on with their education they must move to Lamar. There is a good boarding school there, but not many feel they need to go. Most ranchers think the children are big enough to work on the ranch by the time they are thirteen or fourteen."

Bill said, "You probably noticed we don't have a lumber yard in our town. You have to send to Lamar for any lumber you need to build your place."

"I wondered where the lumber for your buildings came from."

Helen turned to her husband, "Enough talk for tonight. These people are tired and must get some rest."

"Sounds very good to me," Mandy agreed.

Bill said, "I'll go and check the place out, to be sure everything is shut down for the night and get some wood in for the morning fire."

"I'll help you. I want some air anyway."

Helen took Mandy into the bedroom to show her where to put her things. The bed looked so soft Mandy couldn't wait to get her clothes off and into it.

The men came in with the wood.

Zach said, "Well, that'll take care of the morning fire. I'll help you cut some more in the morning. It'll be nice to sleep in a house again."

Zach went into the bedroom and there was Mandy all ready for bed. "Mandy, this is the first time we've been completely alone since we left Springfield."

He took her in his arms and gently kissed her hair, then her eyes and finally a long kiss on the lips. Two very happy people settled down for a long happy night.

CHAPTER FIVE

ZACH FINDS HIS RANCH

The sun was shining brightly through the kitchen window. Helen had breakfast cooking on the stove and Bill had just brought in an arm load of wood.

Bill asked, "Good morning sweetheart. Where's everybody? Aren't the children up yet?"

"I guess Zach and Mandy were more tired than they realized as they haven't come out yet."

"I'll get the children up and washed for breakfast. Hey sleepy heads get up, we've a new beautiful day ahead *of* us."

The sleepy eyed children climbed down the ladder one by one. Little Bill asked "Why are we getting up so early?"

"It's almost 7:00. Do you want to waste a very good day in bed?"

Mark wandered about the kitchen, "Where is Mamma and Papa? Where did they go?"

Zach appeared in the doorway, "Mark, I'd never leave my favorite little boy."

He gave Mark a big hug, "Now, where is my baby boy? There you are, how about a hug for your Papa?"

Zach held the boys on his lap for a while to make them feel more secure.

Mandy stepped into the kitchen, "Oh my, I'm so sorry to be so late. I just didn't wake up. Why didn't you call us? I could of helped with breakfast."

Helen answered, "We both thought you needed your rest. You've had such a long hard trip, there's no hurry as we're not going anywhere."

They set down to a very good breakfast Helen had fixed for them. The children ate everything in sight and wanted more. Mandy said, "Now boys, don't be little pigs. We'll have lunch at noon, then you can fill up again."

Little Bill said, "I guess we'll have to wait until noon for more. Let's go out to the barn and see the baby calf."

All five children Little Bill, George, Cathy, Mark, and Baby Forrest ran out of the house and headed for the barn.

Zach said, "Such energy, I wish I felt like running after a big meal. I'd like to set back and enjoy my full stomach, but I've a lot of things to do."

Helen said, "Why don't you folks take it easy for a few days? We've so much to talk about. We want to hear all about your trip."

Zach answered, "I must get started looking for my land and file a claim with the land board. I don't want to wait. I hear the land is going fast. Finding a good place one must file as soon as possible. I think I'll hitch up the wagon and go into town and see what land is available. It might take a while to find just the right place."

"Wait a minute, I said I'd go with you. Let's saddle a couple of the horses and ride out to the place I found a few days ago. You can look it over and see what's there. It's a lot faster on horse back. This place is about six miles up the creek road. If we go back to town it would take all day traveling with the wagon."

"That would be nice, Bill, but I don't want to take you away from your work."

"Don't worry, my men will take care of anything that needs to be done. I want to go into town anyway. I've some business to take care of. Helen, do you need anything from town that we can bring back on horseback?"

"I don't think so, what we need would take a wagon or buggy. We can wait for a while."

"Mandy, is there anything I could get for you?"

"Not now, I must check over our things, do some washing and get things arranged so I know where to find everything. Maybe I could get some things together so that we can go to church on

Sunday. It's been a long time since we've attended a service."

"I'd like to go to church too. Well, we must be going if we expect to get back by supper time."

Zach gave Mandy a hug and kiss before going out to the stable to help Bill saddle the horses. The children ran up to them, George asked, "Where are you going? Can we come along? I'll get my pony and Little Bill can ride along, too."

"Not today, son," his papa said, "You have guests and must be with them. We're going to town on business and won't have time to look around. Next time we'll arrange for all of you to come with us."

As they rode down the road they waved to Mandy and Helen standing on the porch. The children waved to them from the barn door. The dog, Angel, barked her good-byes too.

It was a beautiful day with the sun shining and the dew was just beginning to lift from the grass. As they rode down the creek road, they talked about the land, cattle, and the possibility of raising grain for the winter feed.

Bill said, "There is a good future in this part of the country. Who knows what a fellow could do with this land if he works hard and plans right?"

"When we get to town I must look around for some horses and equipment to help me get around. I can't hitch up the oxen every time I want to go into town. I'm sure glad I got a good price for my farm. It looks like I'm going to need all of the money I received."

"I'll loan you the use of my horses until you can look around for some real good ones."

About six miles of following the creek, the road became only a trail. As the men rode down the trail they could see open land for miles and miles. Rolling hills and green valleys as far as the eye could see. It was so beautiful as the sun was shining on the far away hills. Deep shadows in the valleys held the dew on the grass waiting for the sun to dry the ground.

Sagebrush and mesquite bushes were everywhere with rocks between each one. The tops of the hills were barren of grass, bushes and trees. Big boulders stuck up like fingers reaching toward the sky.

Bill said, "This is the beginning of the property. Six sections are available, 3840 acres. Right now you can homestead five sections but the river property has to be purchased at $5.00 per acre. The seven acres by the creek would cost about $35.00."

"I think this is just what I had hoped for, plenty of land and close to you. Only six miles from town."

"Let's ride over that rise," Bill suggested, "I want to show you the sod house that somebody left."

As the men rode around the edge of the rise they could see the old sod house. Grass was growing on the roof and out of the sides of the building. All of the windows were broken or missing and the door was barely hanging by one hinge. The men looked inside and it was just as bad. Grass was hanging down from the ceiling and the dirt floor was damp with grass growing here and there.

Zach checked over the building, "This thing is in bad shape."

"It could be fixed up for a temporary home with a little work. You could place some timbers to brace the roof and with planking on the walls and floors it would be real solid. You think about it, and make out some plans. When you build the big house you could use this for your hands. Notice how it's backed up against the hill. That would keep the winter winds from coming in from that side. In the summer the sod house would be the coolest place you could find."

The men rode a ways out into the valley. Bill explained about the land and how things worked on the range.

"This time of the year bunchgrass remains strong and the bluestem grows until the middle of July. As we go further up the rise you will find buffalo grass, as it lays flat along the ground it prevents overgrazing. Grama grass is a short grass of the desert. It grows fast in the spring then becomes dormant, curing up on its roots like hay. Mesquite, sagebrush and chaparral try to choke out the grass but it always comes back in the spring. One thing you have to be on the watch for is the poisonous larkspur, rip gut and cactus. When you run your cattle try to keep these cut back so your animals won't be hurt. The mesquite can be cut and stored for fuel. It makes good heat and the fragrance it expels is wonderful."

Zach was a little overwhelmed with all this information, "It looks like I'm going to have a lot to learn about ranching. It sure isn't like farming in Illinois. I'm not going to give it up, this is what I've wanted to do for a long time."

"I don't know what Mandy is going to say, she wasn't too happy about coming out here in the first place."

"Don't worry. I imagine Helen has been doing a lot of talking while we've been gone. We'd better get to town if you want to make a claim on this land. It's over six miles and then we'll have to come back to my place. We don't want to be late for supper, our ladies would be mad at us."

As they rode along Bill said, "You know this is the way I got started a few years ago. I didn't have as much money as you do, look at my place now. It took a lot of hard work, but it was worth every bit of it."

The men rode back down the trail and following the creek road, they reached town around noon. Bill suggested they stop for lunch at the restaurant. This was a pleasant experience. They talked with several of the ranchers having lunch also.

Bill introduced Zach to the men, and they all welcomed Zach as a fellow rancher.

"I'm not a rancher as yet, but hope to be in the near future."

After lunch the men went to the land office and found the property he was interested in was available. He made arrangements to take over the ownership after he gave them a draft on his Springfield Bank and the land was his.

Bill told Zach that he had some things to take care of and he would meet him back at the hotel. Zach went over to the local bank and transferred the balance of his funds from the Springfield bank to the Chivington bank. As he had a little time before he was to meet Bill he decided to go to the General Store and pick up a few things for Mandy and the boys. Bill came into the store to pick up what he needed, as Zach was making his purchases.

Bill asked, "Are you ready to start home? I've finished my business."

Both men were in a hurry to get back to the ranch and tell the women the news. As they approached the house Mandy ran out, "It's about time, we were getting a little worried."

Zach said to Mandy, "My dear, we've found the perfect ranch, not too far from here. In a day or two, we'll hitch up the wagon and all of us will go out and see what a nice place we have. It's on Rush Creek, a beautiful place. The hills and the valleys go on forever."

"I'm looking forward to seeing our new home. I've been busy getting our things in order so we can find what we need without turning everything up side down."

Zach answered her, "We'll plan on going to church on Sunday since you have things ready. We can dress in the right attire."

CHAPTER SIX

MANDY VISITS THE RANCH

Zach and Mandy enjoyed a few days of rest and visiting with their friends. Mark and Baby Forrest spent most of the time playing in the barn with the new calf and the chickens running around the yard. Little Bill and George had their chores to do, gathering the eggs and cleaning out the stables. When they finished their work they joined Mark and Baby playing with the animals. Cathy didn't play with the boys as she had her dolls to keep her busy. She thought of herself as a little lady and didn't want to get dirty.

After breakfast, one bright and sunny day, Zach decided this would be a good time for them to visit his new ranch.

He wanted Mandy to see the land he had purchased but was a little afraid of what she would say when she saw the sod house.

Zach asked Mandy, "How would you like to visit our ranch? I know you want to have your own place again."

I was wondering when you were going to ask us to go.

"I'll get the boys, I know they would like to go as Mark was asking me yesterday when are we going to have our own yard." Helen said, "We would all like to go. Let's fix up a nice lunch and make it a full day."

Mandy and Helen set about fixing the lunch. Bill went out to the summer house to get a pail of milk for them to drink. Zach headed for the barn to harness the horses to the wagon.

The women packed a good lunch and with the pail of milk wrapped with cold wet rags, they covered it all with a blanket.

Everyone piled into the wagon with Zach. He was a happy man with his family and friends all going to see his new land.

"Mandy, I hope you'll like our place. Some of it's on the creek so there will be lots of water for our stock."

All of the land looked so barren Mandy was not very enthusiastic about what she was about to see. "All right, let's take a look at the wonderful place you've been telling us about."

Zach explained as they drove down the road, "There are no improvements, and we'll have to build everything. That makes it even better as we can put our buildings where we want them. Before we can start building we must have the wells dug and the windmills installed."

Mandy was not as disappointed as she thought she would be as they made their way down the creek road toward the ranch. Cottonwood trees and box elder bushes lined the creek bank. Under the trees lay a beautiful carpet of lush green grass.

Helen said, "The cottonwood trees make such a good shade. Let's come back here for our lunch. The children can play in the grass and maybe go wading in the creek."

A happy group made their way down the road. The children were all jabbering at the same time. The ladies were talking about dresses, cooking and all sorts of household things.

Zach said, "What a noisy bunch we have. Look, Mandy, here's where our land begins. Over that rise there is a little sod house. I thought we might fix it up for a temporary house while we're building the permanent one."

"A sod house, made of dirt! How clean could it be and what are we going to do with our furniture that's coming in the freight wagons?"

Bill answered, "Don't worry, you can keep it in the loft at our place, until your new house is finished."

"That would be a lot of trouble for you."

Zach explained to Mandy, "The sod house is small so I thought we could build a lean-to for a bedroom. A fireplace on the front side would be nice for heat and it would make the place look more like a home. Picture a big rock fireplace with a hearth. With all of the rocks around here it would be an easy job. Can't you just feel the warmth coming from the fire as we sit in our rocking chairs after supper discussing the events of the day?"

"Keep us warm in the winter? Are we going to live in that for months? I couldn't stand it when the sod gets wet, it'll be all mud!"

"Now Mandy, it isn't going to be that way. We'll put in a floor and beams across the ceiling with wood panels on all sides. It don't rain that much anyway."

Bill told Mandy, "The rain's no problem as it only rains hard once in a while, we have only gentle sprinkles. It's the snow that really comes and it's so cold the snow does not melt all at once. The sod house is sixteen inches thick, it will be real warm."

"You fellows have all of the answers. I guess I'll get used to it. I can always go over to Helen's and get clean." They got back into the wagon and Zach drove on through the valley. The grass on the floor of the valley was still green but higher up the rise they went the drier it became. Sagebrush, mesquite and once in a while a cactus could be seen. On the way back down to the valley Zach drove around a little hill. It was a beautiful sight looking over the rises and valleys toward the west.

Helen said, "Oh, what a beautiful view, you could face the house toward the west and watch the sun go down every evening. The sun sinks slowly and as it goes down you can see the shadows growing longer and longer in the valley. Can't you see the beauty of this land?"

"You do make it sound so wonderful. I guess I'll love it as soon as I get used to it."

Bill said, "I'm getting hungry, how about you children?" Mark answered, "Yes, when do we eat?"

Zach turned the wagon around and drove back to the creek. He found a good spot in the shade and the women spread the blanket out for a table. Mandy and Helen se out the sandwiches and potato salad on the blanket along with the pail of cool milk. After they finished lunch the children wanted to run and play. Helen lifted a cake out of the picnic basket. Little Bill shouted, "Oh boy—a cake."

"My favorite—chocolate!" Mark exclaimed.

When everyone had finished eating, the children played on the grass. They would run and hide around the trees and then someone would find them. It was such fun as they didn't have grass around the barn yard.

The women began putting things in the basket, Helen yelled after the children, "Come, we must get back home. It's getting late and Zach has many things to do. We'll come again soon."

As they drove down the road Helen started to sing. Everyone joined in. She had such a lovely voice it was fun to sing along with her.

Helen and Mandy put the lunch things away and started on the evening meal. Mandy said, "As soon as we get things started I think I'll lay out our Sunday things so it won't be hard to get the boys ready for church in the morning."

Bill and Zach unhitched the horses, took them down to the barn. Zach fed them and the oxen while Bill went over to the bunk house to check with his men about the work that had been done through the day.

Zach said, "I feel bad about you taking so much time with us. I sure do appreciate your help and I would like to help you around here for a few days before I go into Lamar for the timbers. I would like to see about getting my wells dug. Do you know anyone around here that does that kind of work?"

"I know just the man to do it. We'll see him at church tomorrow. You can ask him when he can do the job."

"I was afraid I would have to dig the wells myself. I hope he can do the work while I'm in Lamar," Zach continued,

"I think we'd better get back to the house. Our ladies will be out looking for us again."

The men returned to the house and found the women working away in the kitchen. Helen asked, "Are the children in the yard or back in the barn again?"

Zach answered, "They're in the barn with the new calf and Baby is chasing the chickens all over the place. I hope all of the exercise won't keep them from laying."

"I don't think so as they are used to being run around by our children."

Bill told Helen, "We're going to be around the ranch the earlier part of the week to catch up on a few jobs that need to be done."

Mandy answered, "I think that is a good idea as Helen needs to get back to her routine duties. I'll help as much as I can with her work and looking after the children."

Helen said, "The children have had a vacation from their jobs and must get back to gathering the eggs and cleaning up the yard."

Everyone was ready for supper. The children were washed, after playing in the barn they needed a good scrubbing. It was so nice to sit and talk about the events of the day. Mandy talked about fixing up the sod house for a home at least for a little while.

Mandy said, "I'm looking forward to going to church tomorrow. It has been a long time for us. I sure hope Mark and Forrest will be good."

Helen answered, "Don't worry about them. They'll be just fine as there are a lot of children in the Sunday School class. I know they make it interesting for them. The women teaching the class for the smaller ones are very experienced. The regular school teacher instructs the older ones."

After the supper dishes were cleaned and put away, they decided to retire early as they had a busy day.

Mandy and Zach were talking about the events of the day after they went to bed.

Zach held her in his arms, "My dear, don't you think that's a beautiful piece of land? I'm so excited about starting on the sod house so that we can be a real family again. Just you and me and our precious little boys."

"I know you want to get started on your ranch right away. Do you think you can make that awful sod house fit to live in? I love the land and I don't want to live in a wagon again."

As Zach held her in his arms, he gently rubbed her back. This made her more relaxed, and she slowly fell into a peaceful deep sleep.

CHAPTER SEVEN

MEETING NEW FRIENDS

A bright sunny day greeted them as they woke early Sunday morning. While the men were doing the morning chores in the barn, the women were busy in the kitchen. Helen made her plans for Sunday dinner. She decided to put a chicken in the oven now, by the time they returned from Church it would be done. Potatoes needed to be peeled and left in cold water so they wouldn't turn brown. She would put them on to cook when they returned. Helen sent Little Bill out to the spring house for a jar of green beans.

Mandy set about peeling the apples for the pies while Helen made the crust. Mandy said, "Do you have any lemons or lemon juice I could sprinkle on the apples to keep them fresh?"

"Yes, Bill bring a jar of that lemon juice, I think it's on the top shelf. Can you handle both jars? Take Mark with you to hold one of them as you reach for the juice. George, will you go and see what's keeping your Papa so long? Breakfast is ready and we must eat so we can get ready for church."

George found the men harnessing the horses. They had completed the morning chores and were almost ready to come in. Bill wanted to take the buggy but with nine people it wouldn't be big enough so the men decided to take the wagon. Zach swept the wagon and with Bill's help they put in some benches for everyone to sit on. Zach found a blanket for the benches to make a softer ride.

After a hurried breakfast, the women put the dishes in a pan of water to soak. Helen decided they could be washed while waiting for the potatoes to cook.

Mandy and Helen got the children dressed and told them to sit still until they were ready. At last everyone was dressed for Church. As the group marched out to the porch, Mandy said, when she saw the wagon, "This is nice, seats and all. We'll have a nice ride and also look presentable when we get there."

Helen agreed with her, "We'll have a good trip."

Bill drove the wagon so that Zach could sit with Mandy and hold Baby Forrest on his lap. He didn't want Mandy to wrinkle her dress.

When they drove through town, they were greeted by everyone on the street. As the bell in the tower of the church started to ring they drove into the churchyard. People were gathering from miles around, all in their Sunday best. Zach helped Mandy down from the wagon. She looked so beautiful in her light blue taffeta dress with a big blue hat to match. Her hat had a big white feather sweeping across the top and down the back. As she smiled at everyone, Zack thought she was the most beautiful woman in the world.

Zach helped the children down and gave a hand to Helen.

She looked very nice in her bright yellow sheen cotton. Helen had a big yellow hat with a brown feather but not as large as Mandy's. Little Cathy's dress was made of the same material as her mother's but it was shorter. The ladies dresses reached the ground but Cathy's was a little above her ankles.

The men and boys were all dressed in dark suits with very white shirts and black neckties. The boys were tugging at their ties as they didn't like to be dressed up.

Mandy, Helen and Zach walked into the church with the children. One of the ladies at the door took the children to their classes in the basement. Little Bill and George went with the older children and Mark and Cathy found the preschool room. Baby Forrest was taken to the nursery room. He didn't make a fuss as he was the type to make up with anyone. Bill took the wagon around to the back of the churchyard, tied the horses to the rail loosely so that they could move around a bit. He joined the others in the church. Everyone enjoyed the service as the sermon was inspiring and the singing was superb. Helen had such a nice voice, you could hear her above the rest of the congregation. At the end of the service, Bill introduced the newcomers to everyone.

"My friends, I would like to introduce my very old friends from Illinois, Zach and Mandy Denson. They have two boys in the Sunday school class. Zach has made his claim on the land south and west of ours. We would like for all of you to welcome them."

Everyone welcomed them by clapping their hands. Mandy and Zach stood at the door with the pastor to receive their new friends. The congregation gathered in the churchyard to visit.

No one seemed to be in a hurry to get home. The only time they saw their friends was at church on Sunday or once in a while when they went into town.

While visiting with the other ranchers Bill looked around for his old friend, Howard Johnson, the well digger. He spotted him on the other side of the yard talking with some of the men. Howard, a middle aged man with gray hair and beard, he stood tall among the others. A slim man, the lines in his face was evidence of the years of hard work. In fact, he was well known around these parts as the hardest working rancher among them.

Bill yelled, "Hi, Howard, I would like to talk to you for a minute."

Howard walked over to Bill, "Hello, how are you and your family? How can I help you?"

"Zach wants to see you, he needs some help digging the wells on his ranch. We haven't talked to you or Betty since you lost your son. Did you ever find out how the accident happened?"

"Well, as far as we can figure his horse stepped in a rabbit or gopher hole and he was thrown against a rock. He must have been unconscious from the time he hit the rock. If we could've found him sooner he might've come through with just a bump on the head. His horse was lame, and it took him a long time to return to the stable. We backtracked the horse's tracks but it took too long. By the time we found him, it was too late.

I wish I hadn't let him go out on the trail alone. At seventeen, he was too inexperienced. The men that knew the area would be watching for the holes and would know where they might be."

Bill put his hand on Howard's shoulder, "We never know why these things happen. Helen and I both feel your loss and want you to know you and Betty are in our thoughts. How is Betty dealing with this tragedy?"

"She's holding up all right, I guess, at least she is putting up a good front. I think she's over there talking with Helen."

The men walked over to where the women were talking. Betty looked so frail. Wearing the black dress and hat made her look so small and fragile. As the men approached, Helen said, "I've just asked Betty if they would like to come with us for Sunday dinner. I knew you wanted to talk with Howard, and I thought the churchyard was not the place to conduct business, so I invited them. I hope you approve."

As they were talking, Mandy and Zach came toward them with Mark and Baby Forrest in tow. Helen asked the boys, "How was the Sunday School class? Did you have a good time and learn a lot?"

Mark answered, "I like it here, can we come next Sunday?

I watched Baby and he was real good, he sat still and listened to the teacher."

While the women waited for the rest of the children Bill and Howard went to the back of the church to get their rigs. As they walked away Howard said, "We'll follow you with our buggy."

At last everyone was settled in the wagon for the trip back to Bill's ranch. The two mile ride didn't take long.

The men took the horses down to the barn for feed and water. It would be a long afternoon, and they wanted the horses to be comfortable.

Zach asked Howard, "I hope you'll be able to dig some wells for me. I plan for two now and later, when I get my stock, I'll want another one farther out on the range."

"I'll be free this week. Shall we go up to the porch to talk and get out of this sun?"

They talked as they made their way toward the porch, taking off their coats and undoing their ties as they walked. They decided the plans for digging the wells could be made after dinner.

While the men were out taking care of the horses the women were busy in the kitchen. Helen put the potatoes and beans on the stove. The chicken was done and it smelled so good when she took it out of the oven. She placed the pies to the back of the oven so that they would cook slowly. Mandy was busy getting the boys into their play clothes and Cathy out of her Sunday dress. Cathy was happy to put her dress away because she didn't want it to get dirty.

Betty set the table while Helen was busy washing the breakfast dishes.

Betty said, "There is nothing better than hot apple pie." Helen answered, "We'll have a nice dinner and have the rest of the afternoon to visit."

The Sunday dinner was enjoyed by all, even the children couldn't get enough mashed potatoes and gravy. When Helen came out of the kitchen with the fresh baked pies, Little Bill said, "I told you I could smell apple pie. Mamma makes the best pies in the world."

"Don't give me all of the credit. Mandy helped a lot. She made the fillings."

The men retired to the porch to make their plans. After the dishes were washed and put away the women joined them on the porch; it was too hot to stay in the kitchen.

Howard said, "I charge twenty cents a foot. Will drop a six inch diameter pipe in each hole. Sometimes I only have to go down three or four feet, then again three hundred feet. I don't think you'll have to worry about that as you're so close to the creek. I use a forked divining rod to find the right spot to dig. I'll guarantee you'll have water, I'll drop holes until I find it ."

Zach said," "First, I'll have to go over the land and make a decision where I'm going to place the buildings. I hope you can find water close to the barn sight and near the house. I'll go out to the ranch and draw a map of the place, and bring it over to you right away so you can get started. The middle of the week I plan to go to Lamar for some timbers and planking for the old sod house. We're going to fix it up for a temporary home until we can get the big house finished."

"That'll be fine, Bill can tell you how to find our place. The sooner the better as I might get another job. Lots of people are digging wells now."

Helen went to get some lemonade that had been cooling in the summer house. It was a very hot day, at least 100 degrees. When she returned she said, "I hope this will cool us off a bit. Children, don't you want some lemonade? I think you had better get out of the sun for awhile."

"This is so refreshing," Betty said, "I could sit here in the shade forever, but I think we should be on our way, don't you, Howard?"

"Yes, we'd better be going. Zach, I'll see you soon."

The men went to the barn to harness the horse and buggy. Howard and Betty were soon on their way down the road.

Having had such a big Sunday dinner everyone settled for sandwiches and milk for supper.

After they retired for the night Mandy had a difficult time sleeping as she was thinking of Howard and Betty and the loss of their son. A boy only seventeen years old, and now he was gone. She was thinking of Zach and what might happen when he would be out riding alone. What would happen to her and the boys? The country was so rough, a horse could fall at any time.

Zach had no way of knowing the troubled thoughts of his beloved Mandy and she would never tell him. She kept her thoughts to herself. "I'll just pray that we'll all be safe in this virgin land, and Zach and the boys will be able to work the land without being hurt."

CHAPTER EIGHT

HOME CHORES AND HOUSE PLANS

Monday was another sunny day and a person could feel a very hot one was on the way. Helen was making her plans for the week ahead. Monday was always the day to do the family wash. She wanted to start early and hang the clothes on the line before the sun was to high in the sky.

Helen asked Bill, "Will you bring the water in for the wash tubs? We want to put it on the stove to heat as soon as we finish the breakfast dishes."

Zach answered, "Why don't you let me do that, Bill? You can get on with your work."

Bill was glad to have Zach's help as he wanted to ride out to the back range. His men had spotted several strays and they had to get them back with the regular herd. Bill wanted to check the area and see how many men he'd need to do the job.

If it was rough terrain it would take more than just three or four riders.

"I'll stay around here and help the women with the water, cut some wood and clean out the barn. If you need me to ride tomorrow, I'll be glad to help."

"No, I won't need you as I've enough men to do the job. You better get your map over to Howard's so he can get started on your wells and you'll want to get the stakes driven to outline the buildings so he'll know where to dig."

Bill rode off, with one of his men, toward the hills back of the barn. Zach got the water for the women and started on home chores and house plans.

"Come on, children, you can help me stack the wood. We want it to look nice when your Papa comes back."

Little Bill said, "We've got chores to do, gather the eggs first so Mamma can have them for cooking. We'll help as soon as we finish."

"You fellows do your work, Mark and Cathy will help until you are done."

By lunch time, Zach had his work done and the children had completed their chores. He went up to the house to see how the women were doing. He found they were finished with the wash and the clothes were blowing on the line. Zach told Mandy, "I'm going out to the ranch to drive the stakes for our buildings. Would you like to ride along? Maybe the children would like to go too."

"Let me ask Helen if she needs me for anything. I don't know what she's planning to do this afternoon."

"You go with Zach. I'm going to do some mending and make the plans for our meals for the rest of the week."

Zach went out to the shed to get the oxen and bring them up to the house so he could harness them to the wagon.

"It's time these fellows got some exercise. Everyone into the wagon, I've got the stakes and sledge hammer. Just a minute, I forgot my gun."

"Why do you need your gun?"

"Just in case, this is wild country, one must be ready for the unexpected. There are snakes in the unused land and other things, one must be ready. After we complete the buildings and with people around, they leave because snakes like to be left alone. You don't see any around here."

Helen said, "Now you children do what Zach tells you to do, have a good trip and I'll see you by supper time. Here is a little snack and some water jugs. I'm sure you'll get hungry."

Zach and Mandy and all five of the children rode down the road, a very happy group. It was hot but the shade trees made for a good trip. All of the boys and Zach had their big brimmed hats on and Mandy and Cathy had their sun bonnets. The head coverings were necessary to keep out the hot rays of the sun.

The end of the road was in sight, so Zach slowed the oxen down as the trail was going to make it rough riding the rest of the way. They drove past the sod house and on up the hill a little way.

Zach said, "How do you like this spot for the house? The front side will face the west and the kitchen over there. Maybe some day we could fix it so we could pump the water right into the kitchen. Wouldn't that be nice?"

"It'll be a beautiful spot just like Helen said on our previous visit. You can see across the valleys and hills from here. Where are you going to put the barn?"

"Right down there, we want the barn lower than the house because of runoff from the rain and melting snow."

Mark said, "Let me down, I want to see where our house will be."

Mandy answered, "All of you stay in the wagon as there might be snakes around. No one has been here before and the snakes might not like us walking around on their ground."

"Yes, you children stay in the wagon and you too Mandy. I've heavy boots on so they won't attack me as easily."

Zach walked around driving his stakes here and there outlining the foundations. Later when the final plans were made he would be more exact with his measurements.

Mandy and the children were sitting in the wagon and eating some of Helen's snacks when they heard a gun go off.

Mandy yelled out, "Zach, are you all right? What happened?"

"One of the rattlesnakes decided to let me know that I had invaded his home ground. I had to kill him before he could bite me. Now you see why you had to stay in the wagon."

"You'll have to be real careful when you're working around here. There'll be danger all of the time while you're building the house and barn. I'll be so worried."

"We know they're here so we'll be real careful and watch out for them. We'll carry our guns until the land is cleared. After the brush and rocks are moved there won't be any place for them to hide. Now how about some of those snacks and a drink of cold water. It's a mite hot walking around those rocks. I've finished with the stakes. We better head back to Bill's ranch."

Zach climbed into the wagon, turned around and started back to the road. The shade of the trees along the creek bank felt good after being in the hot sun for so long. As they were riding along the creek, Mandy said, "When we get the wells in do you think we could plant some cottonwood trees close to the house? It would make it much cooler."

"We could try, but they take a lot of water and would have to be watered by hand. Maybe we could arrange for the runoff to be directed their way. I'll do some thinking on the idea."

Mark asked, "When are you going to build our house, Papa? It'll be such great fun to have our own place and I can ask Bill, George, and Cathy to come and sleep over night."

"I'm afraid it'll be a while as it's going to take a lot of work. Doing it all by hand without help will make it even longer. You'll have to be patient for a while."

As they drove into the yard, Bill was riding in from the range.

Zach yelled over to him, "How did your ride work out? Are you going to have any trouble with your strays?"

"No, I think we can take care of them with three or four men. The strays found a nice place with lots of grass. We can round them up in a few hours. Thanks for asking, how was your trip?"

Mark said, "Papa killed a rattlesnake. It was this big." Holding out his arms wide.

Helen came out on the porch, "Hello everybody, glad to have you all home. I'll have dinner ready in about an hour. That'll give you time to take care of your chores. That means you, too, boys. I'm sure there're more eggs. The hens have been squawking all day. Maybe they missed having you around or maybe they were telling me there're more eggs."

Mandy said, "I'll come in and help you. Come on, Baby, you can't help with the eggs. I'm afraid you would break them."

Zach and Bill headed for the stables to bed down the animals. The boys and Cathy ran down to the barn to check on the calf.

By the time everyone took care of their chores Helen had dinner on the table.

It was a wonderful meal and all enjoyed the good food after having such a busy day. Helen and Mandy cleared away the dishes and the children went out into the yard to play. The men had papers spread out on the table working on the plans for Zach's buildings.

Bill said, "I think I still have the plans for this place. They're somewhere in the loft. I'll go and see if I can find them."

"That'll be great as I'd like to have a house very much like yours. If you find them, we could use the same specs, we'd know how much lumber we'd need."

Bill came down from the loft, "Here they are, a little dusty but still readable. I couldn't find the ones for the barn. I would guess it would take the same amount of lumber as for the house. The barn is larger but with no inside details it should be about the same."

"I think the people at the lumber yard could give us some information for barns. That's their business and have helped with lots of buildings."

"You're right. Now for the timbers and planking for the sod house. I figure the building is about fourteen by fourteen."

"Yes, about that, but I'll need some extra for the bedroom addition. We'll talk to the lumberman about that also. First thing tomorrow I'll go over to see Howard with the map of the land so he'll know where to start digging."

"Here, I'll draw the route to take to Howard's place."

Having finished the map, he got up and stretched, "I'd better go and see my men about our ride tomorrow. Use any horse you want to ride over to Howard's. We'll be gone by the time you're on your way so help yourself."

"Thanks and you fellows have a good ride."

Zach went into the kitchen and asked, "What are you ladies doing out here? The dishes should've been done long ago."

Mandy answered, "We didn't want to bother you fellows. You had your heads together and were so intent over your papers, we felt we shouldn't interrupt."

"Thanks for thinking of us, but we're all finished now. Bill has gone out to see his men and make the plans for tomorrow's ride. Where are the children?"

Helen answered, "They're still playing in the yard, but it's almost 8:00 and time for them to come in and get cleaned up for bed."

Zach said, "I'll go and get them."

He went out to the porch, and looked all around but no children. He headed for the barn and stables calling as he went—no answer.

CHAPTER NINE

THE LOST CHILDREN

Zach looked all around the barn and went toward the stables, he couldn't see them anywhere. One of the men was coming up from the stables. Zach asked him, "Have you seen the children?"

"They were out back of the stables when they saw a rabbit and ran after it. They followed it up the hill out back. They can't be far as it was only 15 minutes or so since I saw them."

Zach asked the man to come with him to look for them. Bill came out of the bunkhouse and asked, "What's all the excitement about?"

"We can't find the children. We're going to look for them out back of the stables. Your man here saw them a little while ago."

"Let's hurry, there's a lot of brush out there. They're so short they won't be able to see how to get back to the house."

All three of the men hurried through the yard toward the stables. As they were running they kept yelling, Bill yelled, "Bill, George, Mark, where are you? Cathy, please answer us. We'll come and get you."

No answer, only silence. Zach said, "Where can they be?"

Bill told his man to go back to the bunkhouse and get the rest of the men. "Tell them to saddle up and help us look and bring their guns, just in case we see some rattlers."

Zach was so worried, "After seeing that snake this afternoon, I sure hope they don't run into one of them. Why did the children leave the yard? Just this afternoon I told Mark how dangerous it was when you're away from clear ground." "Little Bill, George and even Cathy know better than to leave the yard. I guess they were excited by the rabbit."

Bill and Zach continued looking back of the stables and on up the hill. Zach called, "Bill, George, Mark, Cathy, where are you?"

They kept calling for the children, no answer, Bill said, "How could they get so far in such a short time?"

"Listen, did you hear that? Sounds like crying. Over there by that sagebrush, let's hurry!"

There was Baby Forrest all curled up under a big sagebrush. Zach picked him up and hugged him tight, "Where are the rest of the children? Where is your brother, Mark?"

Baby was still sobbing as he pointed up the hill. Bill and Zach started up the hill as Bill's men rode up on horseback. Bill told his men Baby had pointed up the hill. "Some of you men ride up that way and the rest go around on each side of the hill."

Joe, Bill's foreman said, "We knew you were unarmed so we brought guns for both of you."

Zach thanked Joe as he knew they might need them. They looked for a long time, hours and no luck. They kept calling and calling, they heard three shots.

Bill said, "They've found something. Let's hurry over there, in the draw."

One of the men rode up with Mark on his lap.

He said, "We found him wandering around. He was alone."

Zach asked, "Mark, where are the others? Did you see which way they went?"

Mark answered, "I was looking for the little rabbit, and when I looked up, they were all gone. I didn't know how to get back to the yard, so I just stayed around here. I knew you would come for me or Little Bill would come back. Where is Baby? I can't find him either."

"That was a smart thing to do, just staying in one place. I don't want the women to get worried so why don't you stay with this nice fellow while we find the others. Here, take care of Baby."

Both Mark and Baby had lots of scratches on their face, arms and legs. None of them deep enough to worry about, but they'd be sore for a while.

Bill said, "We have to find them soon, real soon, as it's beginning to get dark. I'll send one of the men back for some torches."

They kept looking with no luck. The man with the torches came back, "The women were at the bunkhouse asking where everyone was. I had to tell them. I'm sorry, sir, they made me tell them."

"That's all right. They had to know something was wrong when we all disappeared. Let's light the torches. Maybe the children will see them and come to us."

Mandy and Helen were standing on the porch at the house. They were worried about their children. Mandy thought to herself, "Oh this awful place, it's eaten up my precious little boys. Why did they leave the yard? Will I ever see them again?"

She walked back and forth, stopping every once in a while to give Helen a hug of assurance.

Helen was very concerned about her children too. "My children never leave the yard. We've lived here a long time, and this has never happened before. Oh, where are our children? All those snakes and creepy things that rove around on the prairie. Mandy, let's pray for their safe return."

Both of the women knelt on the steps of the porch, bowed their heads in silence.

The hunt continued on and on and still no children. As it became darker you could see the lights of the torches all the way up the hill. Then three more shots were heard on the side of the hill.

Bill yelled, "They've found something. Where did the shots come from?"

A rider was coming up fast. "We found them. They said they went up the hill so they could see which way to go to get home. They were worried about Mark and Baby. I told them they were all right."

"You fellows were great, fire four shots so the men will come in. Thank you so much for all of your help."

Joe answered, "All part of the job."

Bill's men took the children back to the ranch house.

Joe said, "We'll send a couple of horses back for you fellows. It's a long way back."

Bill answered, "Thank you. We're both tired. I'll keep one of the torches so you can find us."

As the women were kneeling in prayer they heard the three shots. Mandy said, "Did they find something? Where are they?"

They looked toward the hill, and they could see the torches coming down the hill. Helen said, "Oh, they're coming home! I hope our children are safe."

The women ran into the yard to meet the men riding in with the children.

Finally all were back in the house. Five very tired and scared children and two exhausted men. Little Bill, George and Cathy were scratched all over and covered with dirt.

Bill talked with the children, "I don't understand what made you go into the brush. You know how very dangerous it is with the rattlesnakes, especially when it's so hot and the coyotes come out after dark. They can be as dangerous as the snakes."

The women got busy cleaning up the children. Washing the scratches and putting disinfect cream on them. Some of the cuts were deep while the others were just minor. The chaparral bush was the most dangerous as the thorns could get stuck under the skin and become infected.

Little Bill climbed up on his Papa's lap, "I know it's all my fault. I'm the oldest and I should've stopped the rest from going. I didn't think a little way would hurt. I'm so sorry, and it won't happen again. I was so scared, not for myself but for Mark and Baby. I lost them and didn't know where to go to find them."

As Bill held his son close, Little Bill cried and cried. Zach said, "Now, Little Bill, don't feel it's all your fault. Mark has been instructed to stay in the yard, and he's old enough to know better. In the morning, when we're rested, we'll talk some more about how to take care of ourselves in the prairie. It's past 11:30, and we had better get to bed."

By the time the children woke, Bill and his men were gone. Zach was in the barn getting the horse ready for his trip to see Howard.

Helen and Mandy were ready for their talk with the children. Helen said, "We all have had a big scare, and I'm sure we feel very bad about the whole thing. Mandy and I have decided you need to think about what has happened. We want you to stay in the house the rest of the day after you do your chores. We want you to talk about this with each other and decide how you will act in the future."

Mark said, "But it's such a nice day. Why can't we play on the porch?"

Mandy answered, "No! You stay in the house. That will help you to remember what you've done and why you shouldn't do it again."

Helen said, "Now Bill, George, and Cathy go do your chores and come right back. I don't want to come after you. Do you understand what I'm saying?"

Little Bill answered, "Yes, we do."

It was a very long day for the children and also for their mothers. Everyone was glad to see the men come home. The supper time was very quiet, not much talking this night. The children were made ready for bed and climbed up to the loft without much being said.

Mandy and Helen were tired because of having the children under foot all day.

Bill said, "I sure hope this never happens again. I was really worried."

Helen answered, "I don't think it will. All of the children felt the punishment as well as we did."

Zach asked, "What was the punishment?"

Mandy laughed, "We made them stay in the house all day. I think that was harder on you than the children."

Helen answered, "I think it was. I'm ready for bed. How about all of you?"

CHAPTER TEN

THE TRIP TO LAMAR

Timbers and planking were to be purchased along with the lumber and nails for the sod house and additional lumber for the added bedroom. Window frames and glass were needed for the broken windows. Zach decided to order the lumber for the new barn and house while he was in the lumberyard.

While eating breakfast, Bill talked with the children about the close call they had the day before. "Zach and I have to go to Lamar for a few days, and we don't want to worry about you and what you're doing. You realize the seriousness of your little trip. All of you must do what Helen and Mandy tells you, no running off. Do you all understand?"

Little Bill answered, "Yes, Papa, It won't ever happen again."

Mark said, "It was my fault too. I didn't take very good care of Baby either. I'll watch him all of the time he's outdoors."

Zach said, "Very well, trust you'll do the right thing. Mandy, I hate to leave you with this hanging over us. I think the children know they have to be careful and won't go out of the yard again. We'll have to trust them."

The men went to the barn to get the oxen to harness them to the wagon. Bill brought several buckets with tight lids filled with water for the oxen while on the trip. Helen and Mandy fixed a lunch for them and a large container of coffee to drink as they traveled in the early morning hours. Several water jugs were also stored in the wagon.

Bill said, "We'll be thinking of you and the children and hope everything will be all right. If anything goes wrong, call Joe. He'll help you in any way. We plan on being back by Saturday, but don't worry as it might take us longer. If we're late, have Joe hitch up the buggy so you can go to church Sunday."

Zach gave Mandy a hug and kiss and kissed the boys. As he had his arms around Mandy he whispered in her ear, "I'm going to miss you so much. I love you and don't like being away from you and the boys. Don't worry about us, we'll be fine and I hope the children will be good."

Mandy answered him with a big smile, "We'll be fine, don't be concerned, we'll watch them every minute."

Mandy, Helen and all of the children waved from the porch as the men went off down the road to Chivington. Mandy was deep in thought as they rode away. "This will be the first night that we've been apart since we were married. I'll miss him so much but I do have the boys to watch over and that'll keep me busy. They'll miss their Papa and I must try to make up for their missing him."

Mandy went into the house and headed for the bedroom. She needed to be alone for a short while. On the table, by the bed, set her music box. She opened the lid and listened to the soft sweet sound of her favorite song. She let a tear drop down her cheek.

Mark called, "Momma where are you? Did you go away too?"

"I'm right here Mark, don't worry I had to get something in the bedroom."

She gave him a hug and held him on her lap. She wanted to be sure to let him know he was not alone.

That evening Mandy put the boys to bed with a hug and a kiss for each of them. Now to bed herself. She felt so alone in the big bed she shared with her husband.

Her thoughts were with Zach and his long trip to Lamar, over twenty miles. This would be the first night alone without her loving husband since she was married seven years ago. As she laid down she opened the music box. The soft melody soothed her mind some.

She thought back to the time she was a young girl just past her sixteenth birthday. A handsome young man riding past her uncle's farm caught her eye. A few days later she answered a knock at the door, there he was. He said he had some business with her uncle but she just knew he wanted to see her. The courtship lasted only two months and they were married. The move into the big farmhouse was everything she had dreamed of since she was a little girl. For a few years before she had been working on her hope chest, with embroidered pillow cases, dish towels and scarves.

She thought again about living on the beautiful farm for six years and two sons later when Zach told her he wanted to move to Colorado to be with his good friend of many years. She remembered how heartbroken she had been, but she vowed to love and honor her husband's wishes.

Here they were out west with all of the dust, sagebrush and rattlesnakes. As the music faded away she could hear the coyotes howling on the distant hill. She grabbed Zach's pillow and hung on. She was so afraid, "Oh Zach, don't ever let me be alone again."

As she was crying into the pillow, she began to think of the new house that Zach was going to build. "I must be strong and make the best of all this. I'll work hard to make it beautiful. It'll be a big job with lots of work, but I'll do it!"

As she drifted off to sleep she thought of their friends and how wonderful they were. Bill and Helen were almost like family and she loved them dearly, but she still missed all of the friends she had left behind in Illinois. "I must write to them and let them know we're here and safe."

The men made their way down the road to Lamar, Colorado. It was a long twenty miles, but the road was good. Lamar was the main supply point in the southeastern part of the state.

It was a sunny hot Tuesday, July 1870 and the men were making good time. Zach was thinking of the construction work that had to be done to complete his buildings.

Bill said, "A penny for your thoughts."

"I was thinking of the work that has to be done before I get everything finished."

"Don't worry about that, you'll have plenty of help. We'll have a barn raising party. All of the men in the area will come and put up the main part of the building. We always do that around here. The men work and the women cook. The children come and play planned games. The older children supervise.That way nobody gets hurt and they have a fun time."

"We did that sometimes back home but here everyone lives so far apart. How do they know when it's planned?"

"When you get the lumber we'll make an announcement in church and also post a notice in the General store. We always have a good turnout."

"I would like to get the barn up first so I'll have a place for my oxen. I need a milk cow soon as we need milk for the children."

They rode on, Zach's mind was still working, thinking of the other things that had to be done. When the barn is up and the fencing in for the corals, I want to get started on building a herd of steers. Before the steers, horses and the cows, I'll have to find enough feed to carry us through the winter months. Zach asked, "Do you know if a fellow can purchase feed for the stock around here?"

"You can get feed from several places. There is always someone that has grown more than he needs. You check the General store bulletin board. Something is always for sale, even grain, horses, and all kinds of equipment."

The men continued down the hot dusty road. About halfway there they decided to stop for lunch. The men gave the oxen some water from the water pails. Each of the oxen drank their fill, that would have to hold them until they reached Lamar.

The men set under the wagon to eat their lunch. The sun was so hot they welcomed the shade. It didn't help, because the heat was so intense. As Zach leaned against the wagon wheel, his eyes wandered over the land. He could see miles and miles of rises, hills and valleys. On the top of the hills, rocks of all sizes and shapes. Some were very large, as big as a house and then down to smaller ones. In the valleys, some green was still evident here and there. If this heat kept up the valleys would soon be as brown as the hills.

Bill said, "Looks like we'll have at least another month of this hot weather. It won't be long before the chaparral bushes will break off from their roots and start blowing around in the wind. They blow up against the barn, house and all of the fences. It's always a big job pulling them down and burning them in the middle of the yard. In the open land, they just keep on rolling until they disappear across the hills. All of the time there're rolling they drop seeds along the way, results more chaparral come spring."

At last they could see the town of Lamar in the distance. By the time they arrived, the sun had gone down.

Bill said, "We must find a place to sleep, and I'm hungry. There is a nice hotel down the street and they'll take care of the oxen and wagon."

"Why can't we sleep in the wagon? I've been doing it for weeks."

"I think we'd feel better with a good nights sleep, and it's not safe to sleep in the wagon while we're in town. Someone would just as soon hit you in the head for your money or even your boots. Let's check in and get the oxen settled. We'll have a good dinner. There's a restaurant next door to the hotel." The men had their dinner, just like home cooking. It was still early so they decided to go for a walk down the main street of the town.

Zach said, "It'll be good to stretch our legs and look around a bit. When we were here a few weeks ago, we didn't see any part of the town. We were in such a hurry to get to your place we didn't wait for anything."

Zach found Lamar was a busy town with lots of wagons coming and going, horsemen riding by and many people walking on the street. It had been so hot during the day the people like to walk in the cool of the evening.

Lamar was on the main line of the Santa Fe railroad. The railroad men liked to come to town for the entertainment and relaxation. The drovers and cattlemen also came to town when their days work was done. The men would visit the saloons and stay a little to long. The sheriff would have his hands full trying to keep the peace. In addition to the Sheriff's office and the jail there were several General Mercantile stores, two banks and several dress shops. This being the middle of the week the men from the railroad and the ranchers were not in town. The sheriff could take it a little easier.

The men walked to the end of the street and found the lumberyard. It was locked up for the night. They now knew where to go the first thing in the morning.

Bright and early the next morning, after a good breakfast in the restaurant, they walked down to the lumberyard.

"Good morning," Zach said as they entered the building,

"We need to order some lumber for a house and barn. We

brought the specs for the house with us, but we don't have any for a barn. Do you think you could help us with that?"

The lumberman answered, "Yes, we keep some on hand all the time. Here they are, it shows you in every detail how much lumber you'll need and also how to build it. I'm sure it'll be a great help to you."

"That's good, we'd like to have the lumber delivered to our ranch just outside of Chivington. Can you handle this for us?"

"No problem, but we'll have to charge you for the delivery."

"Yes I know, I had planned on that. We also need timbers and planking for a sod house and some additional lumber to build on a bedroom. We have a wagon to take the timbers back with us."

"You fellows bring your wagon around to the back of the yard and we'll load it for you."

Zach gave him a draft on his Chivington bank and told him they would be back the first thing in the morning.

Zach and Bill took the rest of the day walking around the town. They bought several gifts for their wives and children. After enjoying a big supper in the restaurant they placed an order for a lunch to be packed for the trip back to Chivington They were glad to hear they could have breakfast early as they wanted to get started back as soon as possible.

Zach and Bill arrived at the lumberyard before seven the next morning. The timbers and lumber were loaded and the water pails filled, they were on their way. The trip was slow because of the load.

A few hours down the road Bill said, "There is a turn off down to Rush Creek few miles ahead. Why don't we pull in and find some shade? I think the oxen would like to get out of the sun for a while. There are several trees, and we can have our lunch while they're resting."

"Let's do that, Bill. The rest will do them and us a lot of good."

The men found a nice spot under the trees. After giving the oxen some water they settled down with their sandwiches and a piece of the apple pie the people had put in the lunch box.

Zach said, "I bet it's at least 100 degrees today. Let's stay here for a while before we travel on."

Zach leaned against the wagon wheel and closed his eyes. He

was asleep in no time. He dreamed, thoughts drifted back to his home in Illinois. He lived on the farm his father bought when he was just a baby. All of his life had been good, picnics in the meadow, sitting on the fence watching the horses and cows in the pasture. The best of all, riding his horse after school when the chores were done. His best friend lived on the next farm. Bill was just like a brother because, being an only child, he needed the companionship of a close friend. Years of being together made a bond that couldn't be broken. There were good times, when they became men and after his father died, they worked together and made plans for the future. Bill wanted to go west and become a rancher, dreamed of having a big successful spread in the wilds of Colorado. When Bill moved away, he was lost. His best friend was gone. He loved his wife and boys but he still wanted to be near his friend.

He remembered Bill's letters about this wonderful land urging him to join him out west. Now, he was here and more plans had to be made. He hoped he would be as successful as his good friend. In his mind he could see his beautiful barn full of feed and stock. A big house sitting on the hill. A person could see miles in all directions. The boys playing in the yard and when they were bigger they would ride the range with him. Maybe someday he could take them to a stock auction. Then suddenly Mandy came into the picture. What a sweet, lovable wife she is. He thought, I couldn't do anything if she wasn't by my side. Years of living and loving that beautiful woman will be heaven. Maybe someday we'll have little girls running around the house and helping her as our boys will be with me.

So many things to do, buildings to be built, stock to be bought, feed to be stored. The most important of all, a beautiful home for his family. In time, all of these things will be more than just a dream.

Zach had a smile on his face when Bill woke him, "Are you going to sleep all day. What was on your mind? You sure seemed happy."

The men pulled back on the main road and kept on at their slow pace. At last they arrived in Chivington. By the time they rode the last two miles to the ranch it was after ten. It was a good thing the moon was showing bright. It was like a lantern in the sky. They could see the road as if it were dawn. The women were still up and ran out to the porch when they heard the men coming.

Mandy said, "I'm so glad you're home. I missed you so much. We have some stew on the back of the stove. I know you must be hungry."

Zach answered, "Yes, we're hungry but we must get the oxen put away. We'll be in right away."

Bill asked Helen, "Did you have any trouble with the children?"

"We've been just fine. Everyone was on their best behavior. In fact, they were extra good. I don't think they will ever forget the trip they took up the hill."

Zach reached over and took Mandy's hand, "My dear I missed you so much and was worried about leaving you with the boys."

"We're just fine. You fellows are so tired. Why not talk more in the morning? You need to rest."

CHAPTER ELEVEN

THE SOD HOUSE

Saturday morning the men decided to go to Zach's ranch and unload the wagon. Bill suggested they take a couple of his men along because the timbers were heavy, it would help to have some extra muscle. Bill went to the bunkhouse to check on the work that was done while he was away.

Zach wanted to get a letter written to the freight line so their things could be sent out to them. It would take several weeks after they received the letter for the wagons to reach Colorado from Illinois. He remembered how long it took them on the wagon train.

Mandy said, "Zach, I wrote a letter to our friends back home while you were gone, maybe you can mail my letter too." Bill came in and told Zach he and his men were ready to go.

"We have two letters that need to be mailed. Do you think someone will be going into town?"

The men went out to the porch. Bill saw Joe, his foreman, "Hey, Joe, I would like for you to go into town and mail some letters. Be sure to pick up our mail. Check with Helen and see if she needs anything you could bring back for her."

Joe answered, "That's great, the men were hoping someone would be picking up the mail. I think some of them are expecting catalogs they wrote for."

"When you get back, ride out to Zach's place. We'll need your help."

The men came around the hill, there was the sod house just as they left it a few days before. They decided that the roof was in good shape. They went inside and found it was damp and grass was growing on the floor. Zach wondered how they could build around the dampness.

Bill said, "I guess the rain came through the broken windows. It was a good idea to pick up the windows and glass. When we get the door installed it'll keep the dampness out.

Let's build a fire on the inside of the house to dry the sod before we start to work."

Bill's men started unloading the heavy timbers and planking. They all worked for an hour or two. It took a long time as they wanted to stack them in the order they would be used.

At last the job was done. Bill told his men to start looking for the rocks needed for the fireplace. Zach and Bill started cutting the opening for the fireplace. They let the fire burn inside the house for a while so it would be dry before they started on the shoring.

As the men were looking for the rocks Hank told Bill, "We should've brought the sled out to haul these rocks, they're sure heavy."

"When we come out Monday, we'll bring it along. Our load was too heavy to haul it today."

Zach worried about Bill's men spending so much time away from their work. Bill told him that the work was slow this time of the year, this would give them something to do.

Zach and Bill worked an hour or so knocking the hole in the wall. It was a big job as the walls of the sod house were sixteen inches through. While they were working, Bill had the coffee pot on the fire.

Zach said, "I think we should have some coffee. It sure smells good. I'm getting hungry, how about some lunch?"

Hank said, "That's a good idea. We'll get some more mesquite to keep the fire going before we eat."

After the men had eaten, Zach decided he would walk over to see where Howard had placed the wells. He hoped that he had followed the instructions right so they would have water close to the house and barn. Bill walked along with him after telling his men to rest a while.

Zach said, "As soon as we get the sod house in shape, I'll get started on the stakes for the barn. We can get right to work on the job when the lumber comes.

The men went back to work on the hole in the west wall of the house. The other men spotted several flat rocks for the foundation of the fireplace and marked them with sticks.

The inside of the house had dried out enough for them to start on the shoring. They put out the fire and started hauling in the timbers for the roof beams. This was a big job as they were heavy. The men measured the corners carefully so the timber would be the right length. After sawing them, they stood them up in each corner and then lifted the cross beams to fit on top of the corner timbers. When they were in place they drove large spikes through each one.

This was hard work but at last the job was done. Bill and Zach were pleased with the finished work. They decided they had done enough work for this day. Bill told his men to go back to the ranch and thanked them for working so hard.

The men picked up the tools, put them inside the house. Bill's men rode off down the road. Zach and Bill followed them in the wagon. As they were riding back to Bill's ranch they talked about various things that Zach would have to do.

Bill said, "I know a fellow down toward Eads that has some Hereford cows and a bull for sale. He has them on the range this summer but by fall he wants to sell them. He doesn't want to feed them through the winter months. In the spring, the cows will be ready to drop their calves. If they were yours, you would be on your way to be a big time rancher."

"I'll have to look into that. I want to get started as soon as I get the barn built."

They rode on down the road, Zach was thinking about all of the things he wanted to do. Soon as the barn was finished he would have to see about fencing for the barn area. Stables had to be built, out houses, and at the top of the list was the sod house. A place to live until the main house could be finished. He asked Bill where he should look for the fencing.

Bill answered him, "I think if you check the bulletin board in the General Store, someone will have some for sale. When the work is slow around the ranches, some of the men take wagons up to the head of Rush Creek. They go several miles into the mountains and cut poles just for fencing. The job gives them a little extra cash."

"After the barn is built, I could make the trip myself and save a little money."

"You could do that if you think you have the time. Some of my men would like to go with you if you could pay them a little wage. It wouldn't be as much as if you bought them. When you check the board at the store, you could also look for feed. It's necessary to start stocking up as soon as you can because as it becomes closer to winter the feed becomes less available."

"I wonder how much that fellow will want for his stock?"

"I heard he wants $5.00 per head now, but by next spring he'll want more to cover the cost of the winter feed."

The men continued toward Bill's ranch. Zach's mind kept thinking about the future of his ranch. By next spring I'll need more horses, and I'll need to hire a man or two to help me when I turn the stock out to graze. Another well should be dug a few miles out. On the open range you need water available for each square mile so the stock wouldn't wonder off looking for water.

As they pulled into the yard the women and children ran out to greet them. Helen told that supper would be ready in about an hour.

CHAPTER TWELVE

THE STORM

Helen glanced out the kitchen window as she was getting breakfast started. The sun was a orangey red ball as it came up over the distant hill, proving a very hot day was on the way. Shadows in the valley held the dew on the grass and bushes, it would burn off quickly. The nights were cool, it was hard to think it would turn so hot by midday. That was the way it was on the prairies and in the deserts. She was concerned by the glow of the sun because when the sun was this color it could mean a storm might be on the way. She put these thoughts aside as Mandy came into the kitchen.

"Good morning, Mandy. I thought I'd get a head start on breakfast. Since it's going to be hot today why don't we plan a picnic after church?"

"Oh, that would be fun. We'll put everything in a basket and hide it in the pantry. We can pick it up after we get back. Won't the family wonder why we aren't fixing something for dinner?"

After breakfast Mandy dressed first and when she came out of the bedroom she was beautiful. She wore an emerald green dress with a large matching hat. That made her blond hair even more radiant in the bright sunlight. Dark haired Helen was wearing a bright pink dress and hat. Although the two women were so different in coloring Zach knew they were similar, calm and loving.

"Bill, I think we've two of the loveliest women in the basket with lots of goodies. The children enjoyed playing in the grass and kept wandering toward the creek. Zach told them to stay away from the water until they could go with them.

"It isn't very deep, but you could fall and hit your head on one of the rocks. You might not be able to get up, so be careful."

Mandy watched the children at play and thought what a nice place. They could have many picnics here when it was too hot for them in the yard. Long years ahead of fun watching her boys grow up. As she looked around, she didn't see Baby. "Where's Baby?"

Just then they heard a splash. Everyone jumped up and went running to the creek. There was Baby splashing around in the water. Zach jumped in and grabbed him just as he reached the deep part of the creek. Mandy took him, wrapped him in the blanket and held him tight.

Helen said, "You sure have to keep an eye on that boy. He is inquisitive for a two year old."

After a while Baby fell asleep. The men got up and Zach told the children, "If you take off your shoes and stockings, roll up your pant legs, we'll let you wade in the creek but we're going with you."

There was a lot of squealing and laughing as the children played in the water. After a while the men said it was time to get out and dry their feet. Of course, all of the children objected.

George said, "We want to play just a little longer. We're having so much fun."

Bill answered, "Now be good and maybe we'll do this another day. If you argue with us, we won't plan for any more wading in the creek."

All of them climbed out of the water. As they were drying their feet, they heard a big rumble in the distance.

Bill said, "I think we're in for a thunderstorm. We'd better get packed up and be on our way home. One never knows how fast these storms move. We must get away from the creek because if it's raining up stream the water could get here before the rain. The banks of the creek fill up fast, it would be hard for us to get home."

Everyone hurried around gathering their belongings. At last they were on the way down the road toward the ranch. They had gone just a little way and it started to sprinkle. Mandy thought to herself, "A sprinkle or so won't hurt us. It can't rain too hard in the middle of July."

Bill said, "I think we'd better hurry. I feel we're in for a big storm. When they come up so fast, especially in midsummer, they're usually pretty bad."

They made their way down the dirt road. It had sprinkled enough already to settle the dust. Only a short distance had been covered when it started to rain very hard. The women put the blanket over their heads to keep from getting wet. Bill pushed the horses as much as he could. They seemed to know the urgency of the run down the road. On and on they went with everybody hanging on the sides of the wagon. They were going so fast it made for a rough ride. Suddenly there was a loud crash of lightning, and the horses jumped to the side, but Bill was able to get them under control. He wanted to get to the creek crossing as soon as he could, before the water covered the bridge to the ranch. Finally they got to the bridge, but too late. The water was running over the road and the bridge.

Zach said, "What are we going to do now? We can't take the wagon across the bridge. It's to heavy for the bridge supports."

Bill answered, "Unhitch the horses after we put the wagon on higher ground. We can leave it there until the water goes down."

Another crash of lightning and it started to hail harder and harder. This made the horses jumpy and hard to control. "We can't put the children on these jumpy horses, they might throw them into the creek."

"They'll be all right. Zach, you ride with the children, and I'll walk the horses across the bridge."

Zach got on one of the horses and with two children at a time, he made his way across the bridge with Bill's help.

He made another crossing and then another until all were safely across. It was still quite a distance to go to get to the house. There was no way nine people could make it all at the same time with just two horses. They looked around for some kind of shelter for the balance of the people to stay until they could bring the horses back for them. Bill spotted some rocks with a large overhang, "I think that spot will do as we want them to stay away from anything that would attract the lightning. When we get to the ranch some of my men will come back with us. We can all go back at the same time."

Mandy stayed with the older boys, Mark, George and Little Bill. Bill and Helen rode on one of the horses with Helen holding

Baby in her arms. Zach took the other horse with Cathy riding on his lap.

Mandy said, "Please hurry back as we don't want to be alone too long!"

Off they went down the road. Mandy put the blanket around them and tried to comfort the boys as they were real frightened. She was too but didn't want the boys to know. Mandy and the boys waited under the covering of the overhang. As she was waiting she felt uneasy so she looked out from under the blanket. The water in the creek was rising, and it was almost to the place where they were waiting.

"We must get to higher ground. The water is coming this way! Come on, let's all hold hands and don't let go. That is very important. We must stay together."

Mandy and the boys tried to climb up the muddy hill. After several starts they finally got up the rise a little way. The clay mud stuck to their shoes and the bottom of Mandy's dress. This made it hard for her as the mud was very heavy. At last she spotted a large rock that would give them some cover from the hail stones. It seemed they waited there a long time, but at last, Mandy heard a horse whinny from the road.

Horses were coming! At last they could get back to the house. She yelled at them but it was lost by the sound of the hail. Again and again she yelled and the boys were yelling, too. Still no answer from the road. "Why don't they call back to us?"

The men rode on toward the rock where they should be, it was covered with water.

"Mandy, where are you?" Zach kept calling, "Where are you?"

Bill said, "They must have climbed to higher ground. I'm sure Mandy wouldn't stay here with the water coming up around them. Let's start up the hill. We should go on foot and leave the horses down on the road. I don't think they can make it up the slippery hill. One of you men stay with the horses as they're pretty uneasy."

Zach, Bill, and two of Bill's men started up the hill, taking two steps and slipping back one. They kept on going and at last they spotted the blanket with Mandy and the boys safely hidden under it.

When Mandy saw Zach and the men she said, "Oh Zach! We were so afraid you couldn't find us. The water came up so high we had to leave our spot where you told us to stay."

"Honey, that is just what you should've done. There was no way you could stay there with the water so high. Come on let's go, the men'll help you down the hill."

Zach picked up Mark as he was the smallest and the rest made it down the hill with a little help from Bill and his men. At last they were all back in the house safe and sound.

Helen hugged her boys to her. She was so relieved to have them back in the safety of their home. Water was heating on the stove so they all could wash off the mud.

Everyone was covered with the clay mud, shoes, socks, pants and even between their fingers. They had to use their hands to help them climb up the hill. It took a lot of washing to get them clean and dressed in warm clothes.

Helen said, "The children seem so cold. Why don't we put them in the beds to get warm while we get ourselves cleaned up?"

Little Bill exclaimed, "We don't want to go to bed, it's still day light."

"You don't have to go to sleep. We just want you to get nice and warm. After a while, you can get up, and we'll have a nice supper. How about that?"

George answered, "I'm cold and hungry."

Mark said, "I'm hungry, too."

Mandy answered, "There he goes again, hungry! He's always hungry."

With the children settled in the beds, the women cleaned themselves and started to work in the kitchen. Bill and Zach went out to the barn and stables to see if there was any damage. Zach decided that he might as well forget about going out to his ranch in the near future, until it dried out a bit. The men found several holes in the roof of the barn from the hail but the house seemed to have come through the storm with no damage. They found a small river running from the road to the stables. The water would have to be diverted and channeled away from the buildings.

Helen called from the porch, "Supper will be ready in about half an hour. I was planning a surprise for today but not this much of a surprise."

CHAPTER THIRTEEN

AFTER THE STORM

It was still cloudy when they got up Monday morning. The women were in a hurry for breakfast to be over as they had all the muddy clothes to wash besides the regular wash.

The men were doing the chores and deciding which job to take care of first. The barn had several holes in the roof and a small river was running through the yard toward the stables. This had to be drained off so the yard could dry out. The biggest job of all was to check the bridge over the creek. This had to be done right away because they couldn't get a buggy or wagon across the bridge until they determined how badly it had been damaged.

Bill told some of his men to ride out and check the stock as they might've been frighten by the storm and run off. He wanted them to drive the stock in closer to the barn area and come out to the bridge to help with the rebuilding.

A lot of hail was left in the yard, it would be gone as soon as the sun came out.

Bill said, "Now you children do as your mothers say and keep out of the mud. Zach and I are going down to the creek and see what has to be done to fix the bridge. I'm almost afraid to look at it. Zach, we've some heavy timbers behind the barn we can use for bracing the bridge."

Bill and Zach rode down to the creek. When they saw the bridge, or what was left of it, Bill said, "We'll have to build a complete bridge and even make it longer as one side of the creek bed is gone."

"We're sure lucky to get over the bridge before it collapsed. Let's get back to the barn and pick up the timbers."

As soon as they got back Zach put the horses in their stalls and brought the oxen out of the shed. Bill checked the number of timbers and decided that they would have enough. After hitching the oxen to the sled and loading the timbers along with the tools needed for the repair job, they made their way down the road to the bridge.

After the timbers were unloaded they used the oxen to pull the rocks down to the creek bank where the bridge had collapsed. They had to build up both sides of the bank with rocks so the next time they had a heavy rain neither side would give way.

Bill said, "We haven't had a storm that bad since we've been here. It probably won't rain like that for a long time, but it won't hurt to fix it so it can't happen again. We've got a big job ahead of us. I told Helen to tell the men to come down and help us as soon as they got back. We're going to need all of the help we can get for this job."

The first thing they had to do was to recover as much of the old bridge as they could find and stack it on the side of the road. After unloading the timbers they started collecting the rocks to build up the banks. This was a heavy job and they had to stop every once in a while to rest. As they were resting they heard the men coming down the road.

Bill asked, "How was the stock? You must not have gone very far, you're back so soon."

Joe answered, "They were just over the hill, down in a gully, wading around in the water. We drove them back up the hill where there was a lot of grass. You've got a big job here. What do you want us to do first?"

"We want to line both sides of the creek with rocks as high as we want the floor of the bridge. We'll make the road bed part of the bridge, and if we have enough wood, we can build up the sides. Zach has some lumber coming for his house and barn. We can use that lumber and later we can go back to Lamar and get more if he runs short."

All six of the men worked on hauling and placing the rocks one on top of the other. Some of the rocks were so big it took two or three of the men pushing and shoving to get them in the right place. When the side next to the road leading up to the house was finished, the men had to wade across the creek to start on building the other side. This side of the creek was not as bad so they could do the work without the help of the oxen. It was a good thing as the oxen refused to cross the creek.

The water was still rushing along and it frighten them. While they were taking one of their rest stops, they heard a horse coming down the road from the house. It was Helen in the buggy.

She yelled to them, "Hi fellows, Mandy and I thought you might be hungry so we fixed a lunch for all of you. I brought some extra water tugs."

Zach said, "How nice of you and Mandy to think of us. We're all hungry after this tough job."

Zach opened the basket, "Guess what, men? We've got fried chicken and potato salad. Here is a loaf of bread and chocolate cake. What a lunch!"

The men enjoyed their lunch and were ready to get back to work. They worked for a time and at last they were ready to drop the timbers in place. With two of the men holding them up straight the others piled the rocks around the base of the timbers to make them secure. After adding a few more rocks they felt that the timbers were secure enough to start on the road bed.

The next step was to lay some of the timbers on top of the ones standing and then long spikes were driven through them to hold them together. One of the heavy timbers was placed on the end of the road bed, resting on top of the rocks. The other side of the bridge was done the same way. The foundation for the planking was now finished. They found enough planking from the old bridge to make the road bed but not enough for the sides of the bridge.

Zach said, "I guess we'll have to wait for my lumber to finish the side rails. When we use the bridge, we'll have to be very careful not to run over the sides. Let's get my wagon from the other side. We'll need it when we go back to work on the sod house. I'd like to complete the job as soon as we can. We'll have to walk the oxen across the bridge until we get the sides up. When they see the water they might react and will be hard to handle."

Bill and Zach led the oxen across the bridge. It was a good idea to hold on to them as they were nervous when they saw the rushing water. The men found Zach's wagon where they had left it but the wheels were in mud up the their axles. Bill called to his men to bring the shovels to dig out the wheels.

At last they got the wagon to move down to the road. Two of the men led the oxen across the bridge while Bill followed on foot so that he could check the planking. He wanted to be sure it was holding up under the pressure of the wagon.

All went well and after picking up the rest of the tools and the sled they headed back to the house.

Everyone was waiting for them on the porch as they drove into the yard. They told the women how much they enjoyed the lunch Helen had brought out to them. The children were glad to have the men back because they wanted to make mud pies.

Helen and Mandy made them stay on the porch all day. They were in hopes the men would let them make their pies. No luck, both of them said not today.

As it would be a while before supper, the men decided to just sit back and enjoy the porch. They rocked and talked. It was so nice to be able to relax after working so hard on the bridge. They talked about the storm and of the things that had to be done before the winter weather would set in.

As they were talking, Zach asked Bill, "Do you have any trouble with Indian raiders on the ranches around here? While I was in the hotel the other day, I heard some men talking. They were worried about the Indians and their raids on some of the ranches. One man was telling of the massacre just forty miles from here near Sand Creek. They said that the government gave food and supplies to the Indians but they were still attacking the ranches. Do you think they might come to our ranch?"

"Zach, that Indian war happened over six years ago. Col. John Chivington (our town was named for him) led that massacre in 1864 at Sand Creek. It was a big mistake on his part, and the government tried to make up for it by giving the Indians a place to live and food and supplies. For several years, the Indians fought a guerrilla war, but that has been over for some time.

"In 1867 a peace commission was formed to remove the causes of the war. Government control was set up to secure the frontier settlements, railroad construction, and a system for civilizing the tribes. In November, 1868 a treaty was signed at Fort Laramie with the Sioux's Red Cloud. From 1868 to 1869 the government tried to settle the Indians on fixed reservations two, one in the Black Hills region for the northern tribes and one in Oklahoma territory near Medicine Lodge Creek, for the southern tribes. The Indians agreed to let the whites have free passage through these lands. But they continued to raid because of the lack of food. The government didn't give them enough to live on. Things are better now but there are still a few renegades that left the reservations and are causing some trouble, but not in our area, mostly in southern Colorado, Wyoming, and Nebraska territories.

"One never knows when they will move on to another location. We should be on the lookout for any activity. We don't have as much too lose as the larger ranches. I don't think we'll have any trouble. We must live with the idea that everything will be all right and keep on working to make our ranches successful."

Zach set thinking for a while and then said to Bill, "You sure gave me a head full of information. I guess we must continue working and hope for the best. As soon as we finish working on your barn tomorrow, I want to go out and see how things are at my place."

CHAPTER FOURTEEN

MARK'S BIRTHDAY

Tuesday morning the men were up early to start the repairs on the barn. Bill didn't think it would take too long, with both Zach and himself working, they expected to be finished by noon. He had his men working on the trench to drain the water from the yard. As they were working they heard horses coming down the road.

Howard yelled at them, "Where's Zach? I was on my way to his place and noticed you folks had a little trouble with your bridge. Looks like you did a good job.

Bill was on top of the barn when Howard rode in, "Hi, Howard." Zach climbed down and shook Howard's hand,

"So glad to see you. How do you like the new bridge?"

"Looks like you need more lumber for the side rails. I've some extra with me. You can use it now and pay me back when your lumber comes."

Helen called from the porch, "Hi, Howard, why don't you come in for a cup of coffee? I'm sure Zach would like one."

"We'll be right in."

Mandy and Helen were busy making a cake. Zach asked, "Are you baking another cake? We just had one yesterday."

Mandy answered, "Don't you know what day this is? It's Mark's birthday. He'll be five today. How could you forget?"

"Oh, I did forget! We've had so many things to take care of, it just slipped my mind."

"I didn't forget, and I have a gift for him. So, you needn't worry about it. We're going to have a party for him after we've had our noon meal. It's a secret, so don't say anything"

Bill came in for a cup of coffee and asked what was going on. Helen and Mandy just smiled and said nothing. The men took their cups out on the porch to talk. The storm was the main topic of conversation.

Zach said, "Excuse, I'll be right back."

He headed across the yard to the barn. When he returned he had a small rope with him.

Bill asked, "What are you going to do with the rope?"

"You just wait, you'll find out."

"Howard, how is everything in town? Bill asked. "Did they have any problems?"

"Many of the people had trouble with the big rain, lots of flooding in town. It's good your lumber didn't come Monday as the roads are in bad shape. It'll take a few days for them to dry out. All of the bridges were damaged and some foundations of the buildings have been weakened and will have to be rebuilt. It'll take weeks for things to get back to normal."

Zach asked, "Do you think the ground is too wet to build the windmills?"

"I'm not sure, that's why I was going out there today and take a look. At least I'll have the lumber there to start work as soon as we can."

Mandy came out on the porch, "Lunch will be ready in about fifteen minutes. Helen wanted me to ask you to stay for lunch, Howard, as this is a special day."

"I brought some with me, but a hot lunch would be better. Yes, I would like to stay for the special day."

Bill asked, "What's so special about today's lunch?"

"You'll see"

All the time the men were sitting on the porch, Zach was working with the rope, finally he formed it into a small lasso. Both men were watching him, wondering why he was working so hard on the lasso.

Helen called them in for lunch. All of the children were at the table, washed and smiling. The women had fixed the children's favorites. Lot's of excitement was in the air.

Little Bill asked, "When can we go out in the yard to play? It's no fun just playing on the porch or in the house."

Bill answered, "I think maybe tomorrow, if the sun stays out this afternoon. The men'll have the water drained off by the time we've had our lunch."

Everyone enjoyed their meal and the children were ready to get back to their playing.

Mandy said, "Wait, we haven't had our dessert. Here comes Helen now."

Helen brought in a big chocolate cake with writing on it. It said "Happy Birthday, Mark."

Everyone was surprised, even Mark as he didn't know it was his birthday.

Bill said, "So this is our surprise. Well, Mark, this is your day. You can have the first piece of cake. What do you think about that?"

Mark answered, "Oh thank you, this is fun."

After they had finished their cake, Mandy came out of the bedroom with a package. She gave it to Mark with a big hug. Mark was so happy to have a gift he couldn't wait to get it opened, "Oh, a new shirt for Sunday School. I sure like it. Thank you, Mamma."

"Just a minute I have something on the porch. Here it is, I made it just for you."

Mark was excited, "A lasso. I'll have such fun with this."

"Now Mark, this is for stock, not for people so you leave the children alone when you're playing with it." Zach cautioned Mark as he was throwing the rope around. Mandy said, "Not in the house!"

Bill said, "I'll fix up a dummy cow for you to practice on."

"There is one more thing. Here it is," Helen said as she pulled another package out of her apron pocket.

Mark said, as he hurriedly unwrapped the gift, "A new tie to go with my new shirt. Look, they match. Thank you! All of you!"

Howard said, "That rope will be good for you to practice with, and by the time you get a little bigger, you can work on real stock. Oh, by the way, I think you might like this." Howard pulled a shiny new nickel out of his pocket and gave it to Mark.

"Money, real money, Oh, thank you so much!"

The party was over, and as the women cleared the table, Mandy thanked Helen for her help with the party.

Howard said as he got up from the table, "I must be on my way. Thank you for a good lunch and the party."

Zach said, "Bill, will you need me this afternoon? I think the barn is in pretty good shape. I'd like to go out to my place and see what the storm has done out there."

"You go on with Howard. Tomorrow we can start working again if it dries out enough. My men and I'll work on the bridge. Howard was kind enough to let us use some of his lumber. By the time you get back, we should be finished."

Zach rode off with Howard down the road to his ranch.

As they were riding along Howard said, "I sure hope we don't have any trouble getting up to the wells with the wagon full of lumber."

"It's drying very fast with the sun coming out. I'm sure it'll be hot in a short time. This kind of dirt dries fast and with the grass on the trail it'll be a good foundation for the wagon to roll on.

They arrived at the end of the road and started up the trail toward the sod house. Zach was surprised that it was in such good shape. The only place that was wet was where they made the hole for the fireplace. The planks were wet but Zach decided if he leaned them up against the building the sun would dry them.

Howard had no trouble getting the wagon up to the wells to unload his lumber.

The men worked for an hour or two and decided that they had done enough. As they made their way back to Bill's ranch, Howard said, "I'll bring another load of lumber tomorrow along with my men."

When they got back to the ranch they found Bill and his men were almost done with the sides of the bridge.

Howard said, "I must be getting back home. I'll see all of you tomorrow. My men and I should complete at least one of the windmills and have water pumping by the end of the day. You might think of building a water trough near the well so you can store some of the water we'll be pumping tomorrow. By for now."

Zach said, " Good-bye , see you tomorrow. We've completed most of the shoring, and I think we'll have some planking leftover.

The water trough is a good idea."

Bill said, "We'd better plan on that being our first job. Let's take the sled with us, and my men can start bringing the rocks close in to build the fireplace."

"As soon as we finish the trough, I want to get the door and windows in. The place should be closed in as I want to keep it as clean as possible."

Zach climbed up behind Bill on his horse for the ride back to the house, talking on the way about the work they were going to do the next day. Helen and Mandy were on the porch as they rode in. Zach told Mandy about the sod house and that it was in good condition even after the rain.

Mandy said, "We're talking about going into town tomorrow. Helen wants me to see the store and visit with some of the people in town. Do you think it would be all right?"

"That's a wonderful idea. You haven't been in town yet and there are many people to meet. Bill and I'll be working at the ranch with his men. We won't be back until late. Just fix us all a good lunch and come home when you like. We'll harness the horses to the buggy for you before we leave. Do you think you'll have any trouble with all of the children in the buggy?"

Helen answered, "I've been driving the buggy for a long time and I know the horses very well. Don't you worry as we've told the children where and how to sit. They won't be any trouble."

The children were excited about their trip into town.

Zach said to the children, "Since you're going to town tomorrow, you should have some money to spend. I'm going to give each of you a quarter to spend. You must be careful how you spend it as money is hard to come by and you must be sure of what you want before you buy."

Mandy answered, "We'll be sure they don't waste their money."

Bill suggested, "Let them decide what they want and if it costs too much or not useful suggest they should look around some more. We've had a wonderful supper, and I now suggest we all go to bed as tomorrow will be a busy day for all of us."

Helen said, "You are right. Now all of you up to the loft and go to sleep."

The children had a hard time settling down because they were so happy with their money. They kept on talking about what they were going to buy.

Mandy called to them, "All of you, be quiet and go to sleep."

CHAPTER FIFTEEN

SOD HOUSE REPAIRS

Bill said to his men, "Two of you ride out and check the stock. I want to be sure they're all right. The rest of you come out to Zach's place and help with the rocks for the fireplace. We want to get it built as soon as possible. Zach expects his lumber for the barn and house any day and we want to get the sod house livable as soon as we can.

While Bill was talking with his men, Zach harnessed the oxen to the sled for the trip to the ranch. After the oxen were ready he brought out the horses and hitched them to the buggy so the women and children could make their trip to town. At last they were ready to go. Helen and Mandy came out of the house with their lunch. The children came running out asking, "Can we play in the yard today?"

Zach answered, "Yes, it's dry enough, but remember Mark, do not use your rope on the other children. Try to rope a fence post."

Bill said, "You can rope the post, but don't pull it down." Mandy told the children, "You won't have time to play today as we're going to leave soon."

The men were on their way with Bill's men following on horseback. The trip to Zach's ranch went slow because of the sled. Finally they arrived and started to work. Bill and one of his men got busy on the water trough. Zach started cutting the openings for the windows. He had to make them large enough to fit the frames they bought when they were in Lamar. It was a big job as the existing openings were smaller than the frames. He had to cut through sixteen inches of sod. One window was placed on each side of the fireplace they were building. Then he cut a window on each of the side walls toward the front of the building. He had to place them so there would be room for the door to the bedroom on one side and on the other he had to make a space for the children's bed. As he was working he heard horses coming. He looked out and down the trail, it was Howard and his men coming to work on the windmills.

Zach yelled at him, "Hi, we're glad to see you and your men. Looks like we're going to have a nice day for our work."

"Hello everyone, I'm sure we'll get at least one of the windmills up today and the other one tomorrow. I see you've almost finished the water trough."

Howard and his men went to the well by the barn sight. Zach kept working on his windows. The rest of the men were busy hauling rocks closer to the sod house.

Bill said to them, "Looks like we can start building the fireplace tomorrow. You fellows have been doing a good job. Don't you think it's time for lunch and a little rest?"

The men got back on the job after having the lunch that Mandy and Helen sent with them. It was getting on to four o'clock when they heard more wagons coming down the road.

Zach said, "I bet that's our lumber. I'll ride out to meet them so I can show them the way up to the barn sight for the first drop."

It was the men from the lumberyard. The driver said, "We'd have been here sooner but the roads were in bad shape. We didn't have the rain you folks had. It was dry in Lamar, and we were surprised when we hit the muddy road."

Zach said, "There was no hurry as we couldn't work anyway. Come with me and I'll show you where to drop the first half of your load."

Zach rode ahead of the wagons showing the way. When they got up to the barn sight they found the windmill was up and Howard was hooking the shaft to the wheel so they could start pumping water.

Howard said, "We'll run the wheel for a while to be sure it'll do the job. Zach you'd better come up here so I can show you how to tie off the wheel. That way it won't pump unless you want it to. You want to tie if off when not in use. If a big wind should come up the wheel would break by turning too fast."

Zach made the long climb up to the top to see what he needed to know to control the wheel. By the time he tied off the wheel a couple of times he felt he knew how to control it. The men from the lumberyard finished the first drop. Zach climbed down and rode over to the house sight to show the men where to drop the rest of the load.

When the men finished unloading, they drove by the sod house to talk with Zach and Bill. The driver said, "I think we'd better get back to town. We want to get a room for the night, have some supper and a good night's sleep. We'll be heading back to Lamar tomorrow. I hope you have good luck with your buildings."

Zach answered, "Thanks for the quick delivery and have a good trip back."

Zach had finished the windows and the door was in place. He had installed a split door so they could open the top half for air and keep the lower half closed to keep out any unwanted animals.

"Maybe we'd better get the rocks in order so when we start building the fireplace, we won't have to search for the right size to fit in the right place. Bill, how are we going to seal the fireplace so there won't be air holes between the rocks?"

"Oh that's easy, we just take the dirt and mix it with water and it'll be like the sod house, completely air tight. Here are some good flat rocks for the base and the inside of the hearth."

"How do you make the arch for the inside?"

"The first thing is to pick out a real nice rock, flat on two sides, one side for the front, facing the inside of the room, the other side down toward the opening. We'll build from the outside in. As we get closer to the opening we stagger the rocks. Place each one on the top of the other, hanging over a little, not to much. We'll have to build a frame for the chimney. After we finish with the rocks we can remove it very carefully so we don't loosen any of them."

"I'm sure glad you've done this before, I would have quite a time trying to figure it all out. It sounds like it's going to be a big job."

"Yes, it's a big job but think of the enjoyment you'll have watching the fire on a cold winter night. Let's get going on these rocks. The men have done a good job piling them in order."

"Do you think we should do the fireplace before we do the planking?"

"Yes, you'll want the fireplace in to make a basis for laying the floor. When the fireplace and the planking are done you'll be able to move in."

As they were working, Howard came down to see them, "The windmill is working fine and you have a good head of water.

We filled the trough in a short time. I locked the wheel so the water won't be running on the ground. My men and I are going but we'll be here in the morning to put up the other windmill."

"Thanks for the good job and be sure to bring your bill and I'll have a check for you. Have a good trip home."

Zach, Bill, and the men worked another hour or so and finally Zach said, "I think I've had enough for today, let's go home."

Bill called his men, "We're going home. We'll leave the sled here as we'll need it to clear the land for the barn." "How are we going to get home? Do we have to ride on the back of the oxen?"

"It's better than walking. I'm sure the oxen won't mind." The men climbed on the oxen and started their long trip back to the ranch. Bill said, "Tomorrow we'll ride the horses and lead the oxen as we'll need them to clear the land of rocks and sagebrush."

"That's a good idea, riding on the oxen is not easy. I'll be glad to hear about our families' trip into town. I bet the children will have a lot to say about their adventure."

CHAPTER SIXTEEN

THE TRIP TO TOWN

While the men were working at Zach's ranch the women and children made their trip into town. The children were so excited they could hardly wait to see the stores and the people. Mandy was also looking forward to see something other than the ranch. She felt she had been shut away from people for so long.

They made their way down the main street (the only street) and everyone waved and yelled hello to them. Helen drove the buggy up to the rail in front of the General Store. Everyone got out and walked down the street. Mandy wanted to start at one end of the street and walk to the other end and come back on the opposite side. The children wanted to go into the store at once but their mothers thought they should make their purchases just before they went back home. They were afraid the children would lose their things if they carried them around. Mandy had been in the church on Sunday so they didn't walk up the hill. As they walked along they could see the damage the big rain had caused. Many people were working on the foundations of the buildings. It seemed everything was under control. The first store was the women's dress shop. Mandy was fascinated with the beautiful dresses, hats and under things, all trimmed with lace and ribbons. She felt they cost too much, but she did get some ideas of how she could fashion her own.

Helen also felt she could do better by buying the yardage and doing the work herself. They decided to shop for the material when they got to the General Store.

The next stop was the home of Miss Snyder, the school teacher. She held her classes in her house during the winter months. Since it was summer time she had time to talk with them. Little Bill was glad to see his teacher and make plans for the school year to start in September. This year Cathy would start her first year and she was excited to be able to go to school with her brothers. George didn't want to go to school. He said he was going to stay home so he could play with Mark and Baby Forrest.

Helen said, "Mark and Baby won't be living with us by the time school starts. They'll have their own house out at the ranch. You'll get real lonesome with just me at home."

Mark said, "I want to go to school, too. I'm five now, and I want to go to school."

Miss Snyder answered him "Mark, you must wait until you're six years old, just one more year."

While they were talking Miss Snyder brought in some cookies and milk for the children. She had a fresh pot of coffee for the women. They talked for an hour, Helen said they had to be going as there were many more people they wanted to see.

When they left Miss Snyder's they made their way across the street to the Bank Building. Mandy had met several of the people in the bank at church but it was nice to see where they worked. The owner of the bank, Mr. Crocker, was in. He was happy to meet Zach's wife and children.

Next door to the bank was the sheriff's office. They found Sheriff Mike Wallace behind his desk. He got up to greet them as they came in, "Well, here are our new comers. So glad you stopped by. I've met Zach, and now I know the whole family.

It's good to have new people in our little community. Would you be my guests for lunch at the hotel?"

Mandy answered, "That would be nice, but we don't want to take you away from your duties."

"I have to eat and now is a good time. We don't have much business until the end of the week when the cowboys come to town. Sometimes they get a little out of hand."

As the group came out of the office the stage coach was just pulling up in front of the hotel. The Sheriff excused himself as he walked up to the door of the stage, "I always greet the people when they come into town. Hello folks, nice to have you stop in our town. Are you going to stay awhile?" The Sheriff found the people would be just staying over night as they were on their way to Eads and the others were going on to Denver. After the necessary greetings the Sheriff came back to the women and said, "Let's go in and have our lunch. Are you children hungry?"

While they were having lunch Mandy met several more of the people and also some of the ranchers that were there on business. She had seen lots of them at church but it was good to see them again. After they had eaten the women went on down the street.

One shop specialized in saddles and all the trappings that were needed to ride. Toward the end of the street they found a house that smelled so good. The woman in the house did the baking for the hotel/restaurant. Mandy decided to buy some little cookies and candies. It would be a treat for them all.

As the afternoon progressed they made their way back to the General Store. Now the children were ready to spend their money. There was so much to see in the store they didn't know where to start looking. At last they began to find small things that didn't cost to much. It took over an hour for them to make the right decisions.

Finally everyone was satisfied. Mandy and Helen hustled the children back to the buggy.

When they arrived home, one of the men took care of the horse and buggy. It was only a short time when they heard Zach and Bill coming down the road. They ran out to the porch because they heard the children laughing. There was Bill and Zach riding on the back of the oxen. It did look funny and they laughed too. Mandy said, "That's the funniest thing I've seen in a long time."

Helen asked, "Why are you fellows riding the oxen as if they were horses? What happened to the sled?"

Zach answered, "You just laugh all you want. This is not funny. I don't think I'll ever be able to walk again!"

The children were giggling and pointing at the oxen. George said, "They are sure funny horses, sort of wide for riding." Zach said, "Now that is enough, between you and your mothers, we know that we do look a little funny."

"The sled is at Zach's place. We'll need it tomorrow, it takes too long to bring it back and forth. Don't worry, we'll be riding horses tomorrow. As soon as we get the oxen in their shed we want to hear all about your trip into town." Helen and Mandy fixed a good meal even though they had been gone most of the day.

Bill said, "When we sit down to eat I want to hear all about your trip."

George replied, "I sure had a fun time spending my money. Look at all the stuff I got." He proceeded to spread all of his goodies on the table. He showed a pair of shoestrings, a shinny new marble and a big lollipop. "I even have some money left over."

Little Bill said, "I got good stuff too. See, I got shoestrings and a new comb for my hair. George's lollipop looked so good I got one too but mine's red."

Cathy showed her purchase, "I only got one thing but it's the most important one of all, a new stick doll, see isn't she nice?"

Zach asked, "All of you did just fine, what nice presents. Now Mark, you had a lot of money, tell us about yours."

Mark answered, "I only bought one thing, a new comb like Bill's. I wanted to save the rest of my money, so when I get some more I can buy a new wagon."

Mandy said to him, "Mark, you have a wagon. It's coming with the rest of our things. You don't need a new wagon."

"But I thought our things were lost. They're not here yet. I was getting tired of waiting so long."

Zach picked him up and held him tight and told him, "I wrote to the men with our wagons and I'm sure they are on the way. You know how long it took us to come on the boat and then in the wagon train. You just wait and real soon you'll see them coming down the road. Mandy, what did Baby pick out?"

"Baby couldn't keep his eye off a tiny wagon, not more than three inches long. I think he'll have a lot of fun with it. Bob, the store owner said a man hand carved it. He carves toys all of the time. We must think about that for Christmas gifts for the children."

Bill said, "Now the children have showed us their presents, what do you ladies have to show for your trip?"

Helen answered, "We did just fine, I'll show you. I have my things in the bedroom."

Helen came out with a bolt of cloth, thread and some feathers.

All of them the same color. She said, "I think they'll make a handsome outfit, don't you?"

"What a nice picture you'll make at church."

Zach asked, "Mandy let us see what you have."

Mandy went into their bedroom and brought out a big bag. It seemed heavy when she carried it to the table. She pulled out skeins and skeins of yarn. All colors, white, red, blue, yellow and brown.

"What are you going to do with all that yarn?"

"First of all, I'm going to make me a new white shawl to wear to church when the weather turns cooler. The rest I'm going to knit into sweaters for all of you. I need hand work after the chores are done at the end of the day."

"Mandy, you're always thinking of others. Why didn't you get some material for a new dress? You need a new one as the others you've had a long time."

"Zach, quit your fussing. When the time is right I'll get some material. Oh by the way, we picked up the mail while we were in town. It's somewhere at the bottom of the bag of yarn, here it is."

Bill took the package of mail and sorted it into stacks. Some for the men he had working for him, some for him and then he said, "Look two letters for you folks, one to Zach and one to Mandy."

Mandy said, "I hope it's from my friends back home. I can't wait to see what they have to say. I've had no news since we left home."

Mandy took her letter over to a chair in the far corner of the room so she could read it alone. She knew she might cry while reading about the people she dearly missed.

Zach opened his letter and exclaimed, "It's from the freight line and they say our wagons left. Wait let me check the day they left, three weeks ago. They went by the way of the Old Santa Fe Trail. He says he thinks it'll take them about six weeks. Mandy, that means we'll have our things in about three more weeks. Isn't that great?"

Mandy answered, "I'll be so happy to have my beautiful things with me again. Did you hear that Mark? Your wagon is coming in just a few weeks."

"Oh that's great, my own wagon to play with!"

Helen said, "That's wonderful, your own things. I know how

long I waited for mine, It seemed forever."

"That means we'll have to put our backs into our work so we'll have a place for your beautiful things. Bill, tomorrow is Saturday so I guess we'd better write that notice for Bob to put up in the General Store about our barn raising. What do you think of a week from next Wednesday? That would give us time to plan on the party, get the ground cleared and all of the other things we'll need to do."

"We'll do it tomorrow. We can pass the word to everyone at church. We're going to have a barn raising! Then in a couple of weeks we'll have another, a house raising!"

Mandy said, "You mean the time has come we'll have our own home again. Helen and Bill, you people have been so good to us, letting us live with you and everything."

"We enjoyed having you and I personally like having a woman around to help with the house work. Now, my dear, you'll have your own work to do. Setting up a house from the top down is a very big job. It'll be fun placing your own things in your own home."

The men sat at the table writing the notice they were going to give to Bob to be posted in the General Store.

The men made their plans for the week. What job should they do first? They decided the fireplace should be the first one. It wouldn't take long to finish the paneling and start on the bedroom. The windows and door were in but they would have to cut another hole in the wall for the door to the bedroom. That would take a while. Bill said he would have all of his men come out and help so they would get done in plenty of time.

CHAPTER SEVENTEEN

THE WORK CONTINUES

All of the men were out at Zach's ranch working. Zach mixed the mortar of dirt and water to be used in the fireplace. He made it very thick (like mud). Bill and some of the men were working on the floor of the sod house. It had to be made level so when the planks were laid there wouldn't be any high spots. The men were so busy they didn't hear Howard coming with his men.

Howard said, "Hi, everyone is sure busy. With all of this activity you'll be done before you know it."

Zach said to Bill, "You know these fellows have been working hard this week. What do you say about letting them off work early today, about three? That way they can get home, cleaned up and have a night out. After all, it's Saturday."

"That's all right with me. It has been so long since I was a single fellow. I forgot they need some time to play. Hey fellows, Zach says he wants to let you off about three so you can go into town if you want to."

Joe said, "That's great, thanks a lot."

The worked continued. He had his men hitch the oxen to the sled and go up to the barn sight to clear the land. They used picks and shovels to dig the sagebrush and mesquite bushes. They piled the mesquite to one side as they wanted to save it for fuel. The rocks were pulled to the back of the barn area.

As the fireplace began to take shape, Bill said it was time to build and place the wooden frame for the chimney. It had to be thirteen feet tall and extend three feet above the roof of the sod house. They placed it on the base of the firebox and up through the center of the fireplace. The rocks extended one foot on the inside of the house, sixteen inches through the width of the sod and eighteen or twenty inches on the outside of the building.

The fireplace was looking better with each stone.

Zach said, "Why did you want to save the special flat sided rock, how are we going to use it?"

"We'll use it as the hearth stone over the top of the opening of the firebox. That is the tradition when making fireplaces."

"I've never heard of that but it sure sounds interesting. I'll have to look very carefully for a stone for the house. I expect to live in that house for a very long time."

Bill and Zach continued their work and at last they started the curve toward the center. They picked out each rock very carefully so that it would match the one before it. The rock had to be the right size and also the right color to match as close as they could. Finally they reached the center, making sure each rock placed was secure before they placed the large hearth stone on top of them. At last the arch was complete. Bill said, "That is the hardest part of the whole job. The rest won't have to match so closely, and it'll go fast. We'll rig up some kind of ladder as we go higher. Thirteen feet can't be reached from the ground."

"Why don't we use the wagon? It would give us the extra height we'll need. Let's bring it out Monday and try to use it before we build a ladder." The men kept on building until it was eight feet wide and at least three feet through. It would be a way to go before reaching the tallest point. Twelve inches above the roof they would have to start tapering in a little at a time. The actual opening for the chimney would only be three feet by two feet.

As they were working, Howard came over, "Aren't you fellows going to stop for lunch? We're getting along fine but have a little more to do before we finish the job."

Bill said, "I'm glad you stopped us. We just got carried away with our work. Zach, I think we'd better rest a while and have our lunch."

"I didn't realize how hungry I had become, let's eat! I wonder how the boys are doing with the barn sight? After we eat, let's ride over and see. I'm sure it'll take a few days as there's lots of rocks in this part of the valley."

Zach and Bill rode over to the barn site. Howard went back to where they were building the windmills. When the men got to the site they were pleasantly surprised to find the men were over half done with the clearing.

Bill said, "You fellows sure have been working hard. Didn't you take a lunch break?"

Joe answered, "We figured we'd keep on the job since we're leaving early. We'll eat on the way back to the ranch."

"You fellows should've taken a break. You'll be too tired to have fun tonight."

"No way, we'll have a real good time!"

Zach and Bill went back to work on the fireplace. They decided to make the firebox thirty inches deep. That way a larger fire could be built without being too close to the front opening. As they continued working they heard the men coming back with the oxen.

Joe said, "We left the sled at the sight to be used on Monday. We think the oxen have worked enough for today, they seem a little tired. Thanks for the time off. We'll see you later at the ranch."

Zach and Bill worked another hour or so and Howard came with his men. "Zach you're ready to go. I tied down the wheel so you won't have to check it. We'll see you in church tomorrow. Bye for now."

Long about five they decided they would call it a day. The men put all the tools inside the sod house and closed the door. Since they hadn't put the locks on the doors, they had to fasten them with a rope so they wouldn't blow open. The oxen were put on a lead so they could follow the horses without too much trouble.

CHAPTER EIGHTEEN

SUNDAY OUTING

Zach said, "Why don't we ride out to the ranch and let you and the children see the work we've done? After church we'll have a little lunch and go for a ride."

Mark replied, "Oh great, we want to see the windmills and everything"

Cathy said, "Can I take my new doll to see the ranch?"

Bill said to her, "That's fine but don't lose her in the big wagon!"

The church service was as good as usual. At the end of the service Zach made his announcement regarding the barn raising party. "We'll be ready for the barn raising party one week from next Wednesday. We want you and your families to come for work, food, and games for the children. Please sign up at the General Store, Bob will have the sheet. I hope you ladies will honor us with your best dishes."

The children were anxious to get home, have their lunch and see the ranch with the windmills, the house and all of the cleared ground they planned to play on.

Mandy said to Zach, "My dear, you've been working so hard, I know I'll like everything you've done on the sod house."

As they reached the end of the road they could see the windmills high in the sky. The children were so excited. Little Bill said, "Oh look, see how tall they are!"

Everyone got out and went into the house. Mandy was very impressed with the fireplace. "Look how big it is. The rocks are all the same color. This makes the room so much more like a real house. The windows let in a lot of light. I like the way they are set on the inside wall. In the spring and summer I can sit flower pots on the outside ledge and they can be seen from the inside of the house. Helen, wouldn't bright colored curtains look nice? I must get to work right away making them so they will be ready when we move in."

"Oh, Zach, how thoughtful of you to make the split door. I can keep the top half open to watch the children playing in the yard. With the lower half closed it would keep the chickens and other things out in the yard where they should be. Will we have a window in the bedroom? If we do, I'll have to make curtains for it also."

Zach answered, "We'll build the bedroom on that side of the house as soon as we complete the paneling and floor." The children wanted to run around in the yard.

Bill said, "We haven't cleared the ground around the house yet so it's not safe to go into the yard until we get that taken care of. We'll get it done real soon."

They rode on to the barn sight and because much of this part of the land had been cleared they let the children out of the wagon. They ran up to the water trough and immediately started throwing water at each other.

Mandy said, "Look at that, water everywhere and mud on their shoes. I think it's time to get into the wagon and head for home. We didn't have much for lunch so we'd better prepare a good supper."

They headed back to Bill's ranch to get the children cleaned up and start supper. Everyone was so happy with the work and how nice the fireplace was shaping up. As they rode along, they talked about the weeks to come.

Zach said, "Next week we should have everything ready for the barn raising. I must get the stakes driven so we'll know where to start."

"Zach, are we going to be able to get some kind of stove for the sod house? We'll need one for cooking and to heat water to wash the dishes."

Bill answered, "We'll have Bob ask around for a used stove. You'll only have to use it a short time as your good one will come with your furniture."

While Bill was doing the evening chores he talked with his

men. He asked about their trip to town the night before.

"Did you fellows have a good time? You all worked so hard this week I sure hope you did."

Joe answered, "Yes, we did real well until we got in a poker game. Some of the fellows did pretty good for a while. There was a fellow in the card room, we've never seen him before. He was a stranger to everybody. Well, he started playing with us, and before we knew it, he took all our money."

"It was getting pretty late so we just wanted to head back to the ranch. We didn't have any more money to drink or play. As we were leaving, we ran into Sheriff Mike and told him what happened. He said he had heard about our bad luck, and he was wondering how it happened as he had played with us and knew we were good card players. He also said he was going to check on this fellow and find out where he came from and how long he was going to stay. He said he didn't want anyone making trouble in his town. It has always been a quiet town with just the ranchers and their men enjoying their free time without a hassle. Then we came on home with a headache and empty pockets."

Bill told him how sorry he was they had such a bad night. "I hope Sheriff Mike finds out about this fellow and sends him on his way. We don't want that kind of person in this part of the country."

CHAPTER NINETEEN

FINISHING THE SOD HOUSE

Zach and Bill both felt this week would be the beginning of the end in preparing the land for the buildings. After Bill's men finished the land for the barn they began clearing the brush around the house, piling the mesquite in one area and the rocks in another.

Bill said, "Fellows, when this area is cleared you can start over there where Zach wants his house. When that's done, we'll have lots of room for the wagons and animals for the big party. We want all of you to come to the party, you have done so much of the work making it all possible."

Zach and Bill continued building the fireplace and with the help of Zach's wagon, they were able to reach the top of the chimney. When the job was done, both men stood back and admired their work. They couldn't tarry long as there was still a lot of work to be done before they could say the job was finished.

Zach opened the windows and the door so they could have more air while working on the inside of the building. The men decided that the paneling for the ceiling and walls should be placed before the flooring. On the right side wall they had to cut an opening for the door to the bedroom he was to build. After they cut the hole, Zach made a door frame but he didn't have enough lumber for the door.

"When we get the walls in and the floor laid I might find enough left over for a door. Since it'll be an inside door it won't have to be as heavy as the other one."

The men worked all day on the ceiling. It was hard work trying to match the panels so there would be no cracks to let the dirt from the sod to slip through.

Along about five they decided they had worked enough for the day. Bill called to his men, "Looks like you might finish clearing the land tomorrow. You'll be glad to get back to your regular work, riding after the stock. No telling where they are now as we haven't given them much attention lately."

The next day, all of the men returned to Zach's ranch to continue their work. "You know, Bill, we need to make a hole in the ceiling for the stove pipe."

"Let's do it first and then we can finish the ceiling."

Cutting through the roof was just as difficult as the walls. It wasn't as thick but real hard. They finished the hole and continued working on the ceiling. At last it was finished.

Zach said, "That sure looks good, I hope the side walls will go a little faster. After we get a good start on the walls, can you keep going by yourself? I would like to start on the bedroom, at least get the frame together."

"That's a good idea, I'll get to work."

The men continued with their jobs. By noon Zach had most of the framework completed and Bill was almost finished with the paneling. They stopped for lunch and rode over to where the men were clearing the land. Everything was looking good.

Bill asked, "You fellows are doing a good job. Have you had much trouble with rattlers?"

Joe answered, "We've found a few under the rocks. They wanted to keep out of the sun. We did away with all we could find."

"That's good, we wouldn't want anyone to get bitten while we're having our party. Joe, we'd like you to go into town and post this notice at Bob's store. We're looking for a good used cooking stove for the sod house. It should be in pretty good shape as later the hired hands will be using it for their meals."

"I'll get started right away and pick up the mail while I'm in town. See you back at the ranch."

Zach and Bill went back to work in the sod house and the men continued clearing the land. The day progressed and finally it was time to quit.

Zach said, "This was a good day's work. Let's go home and take it easy. I feel like sitting on the porch and watching the sun go down. How about you?"

"Let's go!"

On Wednesday Bill and Zach had the men help them raise the frames of the bedroom and nail them together. Now for the roof, this was an easy job, but it was very hot.

Zach thought, "This is going to be one of the hottest days we've worked."

"I think it's going to be over one hundred degrees today. Let's finish the roof in the morning before it gets to hot. We can lay the floor as it'll be much cooler inside."

They worked the rest of the day laying the floor. It was an easy job as the boys had the floor level and the boards fit together just right. They had to make cutouts for the fireplace and the door openings.

Bill said, "Let's put things away and get back to the ranch ourselves. We don't want to overdo in this heat."

"I think we can finish up most of the outside work on the bedroom in the morning."

They headed back to the ranch. Bill decided he could get caught up on some of the chores around the barn.

Helen and Mandy were glad to see them when they rode into the yard with the oxen and wagon.

Mandy yelled at them, "Zach, I want to tell you what Joe said when he came back from town."

"Right now? We want to give the oxen some water and feed as it's been so hot today."

Bill said, "You go ahead. I can take care of them."

Mandy told the men, "When Joe got into town to put up the notice he found someone had already put up a notice saying they had a stove for sale. The people live right in town. Can we go and see it tomorrow? I'm real anxious to get one in the house before next week."

"Well I guess we could use a day of rest. We've been working so hard, and I'm sure Bill needs to take care of some things around here."

So, it was decided, tomorrow they would go into town. The children were happy to be able to go again.

Mandy and Zach went into town the next day and Bob told them where the people lived that had the stove for sale. They had no trouble finding the right house and the people were glad to see them. They had been saving for a long time so they could buy a new stove. The woman was happy to show Mandy her new shiny stove.

She said, "We've the old one on the back porch. Come, and I'll show you. It works just fine as I've used it a long time. It cooks real good and doesn't take much fuel to keep it hot."

"It looks good. I'm sure Zach will think so too."

The men loaded the stove. When they got back to the ranch, Zach asked Bill if he could have two of his men help him unload the stove.

While they were in town, Zach picked up extra pipe so they would be sure to have enough. He wanted to make it a double pipe so the panels in the ceiling wouldn't get too hot.

The men got the stove in place and connected the pipe. It worked just fine.

Zach said, "Well, now all we'll need is some furniture."

They went back to Bill's place. Mandy was waiting on the porch.

Zach told her, "I think it's going to be cooler tomorrow, and we can finish the roof. Bob gave me a list of people that signed up for the barn raising. Look's like we'll have a good crowd. I had better make some tables and benches so they'll have a place to sit and eat. We can break them up and use the lumber later if we need it."

Friday the men rode out to finish the roof and do the paneling in the bedroom. It wouldn't be long before the house would be ready to move into as soon as they completed the flooring.

Zach said. "You know we forgot something very important. We'll need to dig some holes for the outhouses and put the buildings together. We'll have a lot of people here next Wednesday, the outhouses will be needed."

"Let's dig the holes in the morning when it's cooler. We can go ahead and build the outhouses and then place them when we get the holes dug. How many do you want?"

"We'll need one near the sod house, not too close to the hill as the rattlers might find it a cool place to be. The men have cleared a good spot. We'll want another one near the house and one near the barn. They should be about four or five feet deep, we can keep throwing a little dirt in them."

"That's going to be a big job, I think I'll have two of my strongest men come out and help in the morning. With all of the rocks they'll have to use picks and shovels to get the depth we want."

They spent the rest of the day building the outhouses and placed them near the spot where the holes would be, so they wouldn't have to move them too far. This was an easy job as the buildings were small.

Saturday, at first light, the men were on their way. They wanted to get the holes dug before it became too hot. After several hours on the job, they had completed only two of the three. They placed the houses over the holes and made a little step up to the door as the ground was uneven.

Zach said, "I think we'll let the other one go until later as it's getting too hot to work. One by the barn and the other by the sod house will do for now."

"You fellows have done a good job. You can go back to the ranch. That's enough work for today. Are you going into town tonight? Maybe you could get some of your money back." Hank said, "I don't think I'm going to take a chance on losing the money I've got in my sock. I don't know about the others, but I'm going to wait until that guy leaves town. I hope Sheriff Mike got rid of him."

"I hope so too, we don't need that kind around here. Zach, let's get things put away and head back ourselves. This has been a good week's work. Tomorrow will be a day of rest."

CHAPTER TWENTY

THE BARN RAISING

Almost everyone they talked to after Church on Sunday said they were going to come to the barn raising on Wednesday. On the way home Zach said, "Let's all go out to our ranch this afternoon. I want to show you and Helen all of the work we've done. I also want to pick out some of the lumber and get it ready to make the tables and benches first thing in the morning.

After lunch everyone was ready for the trip to the ranch.

As Zach drove the wagon up to the sod house, Mandy said, "Look at the fireplace! Isn't it beautiful? I can't wait to see inside, Oh, look at the bedroom! Let's go inside and see the stove and the fireplace from the inside."

They all climbed out of the wagon and rushed inside to see the work that had been done. The children started to run around the yard. Bill yelled to them, "Stay away from the rocks as there might be some snakes around, and we don't want anyone bitten!"

Helen remarked, "Oh how nice everything looks. Just look at the paneling. You fellows have sure done a nice job, this is really a livable place."

Mandy said, "The stove looks great! I think I could cook up some good meals on this. Look, Helen, it has a place to keep water on the side, we can have warm water without putting a pot on the stove."

"I've seen this before, I think it's called a reservoir. Just think, you'll always have hot water!"

Zach said to Bill, "Do you think we could take the wooden

frame out of the fireplace? I could use the boards for some of the tables."

"Maybe we had better wait until tomorrow or the next day as we want to be sure the mortar is set real tight."

After they inspected the house, Zach headed the horses back to Bill's place. While the women were getting supper together, Bill and Zach were playing with the children. Bill found two more ropes and made lassos for Little Bill and George. Now all of the boys except Baby had ropes to play with. He made a make-believe cow out of some straw and burlap. The men spent a lot of time showing the boys how to rope the make-believe cow.

Zach went out to his ranch alone on Monday to make the tables and benches for the party. When he finished he drove the stakes for the outline of the barn. Everything seemed to be falling into place and he was pleased with the outcome of their labor. As he did his work he was thinking, "I should go into town and see if I can find a metal water trough as the wooden one won't be near big enough for the animals we're expecting at the barn raising."

Zach went back to Bill's ranch and told Mandy, "I'm going to ride into town and look for a metal water trough to place near the windmill by the barn. That wooded one is not near big enough. Do you want anything from town?"

"I'm glad you're going into town as there are a few things we need from the store. I have a list and I was hoping someone would be going, I'm glad it's you."

"I'm taking the wagon, so if you need any flour or big items, I'll have room for them."

Zach took the list and was on his way. When he saw Bob at the store, he found he had two water troughs on hand. Zach decided to get both of them so when the other well was dug he would have it ready to use. He picked up the things on Mandy's list and the mail. He was glad he decided to come today as now he could get the troughs in place Tuesday and filled with water for the animals coming on Wednesday.

When he got back to the ranch he found the women had been busy cooking for the Wednesday party. They had a big pot of beans cooking on top of the stove. Potatoes and onions were all laid out for the potato salad and a big chocolate cake was sitting on the counter.

Zach remarked, "Look's like you've everything ready. What are you going to do tomorrow?"

Helen answered, "We're going to fry up two or three chickens. We're going to have fried chicken with the beans and potato salad."

"Sure sounds like we'll have plenty to eat."

Zach left early Tuesday morning to take his tanks out to the ranch. He was so happy his ranch was at last taking shape When the barn was built he could start looking for stock and feed for them. Of course it would take a lot of work to finish the barn after the main frame was completed. He wanted to outline the area for the fence around the barn area with rocks. This would make it attractive.

After leveling the ground he dumped one of the tanks. Each tank had a spout that could be turned off and on. He made sure the spout was on the downward side so it could be drained without any trouble. After he had the tank in place and the spout turned off he climbed to the top of the windmill and loosened the wheel. Almost immediately the water started to fill the tank. Zach stood back and smiled. This was the beginning he had waited for such a long time. The water was coming so fast he had to wait until the tank was almost full, then he fastened the wheel so it wouldn't pump any more water. He went over to the other windmill and followed the same process. At last both tanks were full. He headed back to Bill's ranch a very happy man.

As he passed the house on the way to the barn he could smell fried chicken cooking in the kitchen. Bill was in the barn and said, "Hi, how did it go? I hope you didn't have any trouble with the tanks."

"Everything is fine. I filled the tanks and it didn't take very long as I had a good head of water. I'm so pleased with everything and I don't know how I'll ever repay you for all your help."

Bill answered, "Well, we're good friends and out in this part of the world everybody helps everybody. Your turn will come, just wait and see. I've got my work all done. What do you say about helping the boys with their roping?"

"That's a good idea, I'm sure they would like a little help."

At last it was Wednesday, the big day had arrived. Everbody

was so excited, the women loaded the food and water jugs in the wagon. All of the children climbed in with the things they were going to use in the games their mothers had planned.

They arrived early before the others so they could direct them where to place their wagons. Zach decided that a circle would be a good idea, just like they did on the wagon train. With all the wagons in a circle, they could keep the animals inside with their food and none of them would stray away. Once in a while someone could take them up to the water tanks for a drink.

The women took the food inside of the sod house to keep it cooler. They were so happy to have a social gathering as they didn't have a party very often. The men started to work right away. Zach figured there were about forty five or fifty men working all at once.

Zach spread the specs out on one of the tables so the men could read the measurements in order to know how long they would have to cut the lumber. Cutting and hammering, lifting and carrying the lumber progressed hour after hour. Some of the men placed the large timbers upright at each corner and every ten feet apart on the inside edge and in the center.

This would give the men something to nail the outside frame to. At last one side was completed. It took a dozen men all together to lift the completed side to an upright position. As the men held it upright several others were nailing and bracing it in place. At last it was up and solid. The men gave a big yell! Now to start on the other side. The work went well and in another hour it was completed. Two more sides to go and Zach said to the men, "You fellows have done a real good job, don't worry about the windows and doors as I can do them later. I think it's time for lunch. I just passed by the tables and I'm sure you're in for a real treat!"

After the men had their lunch and a little rest they got back to work. While the men were working the children were having a good time with their games. They had a three legged race, a game where they had to carry an egg on a spoon for fifteen feet without dropping the egg. They also had a tag game that made everybody laugh. The women let the older children supervise the games while they took care of the food. Mandy had a fire in her stove and made coffee for all. She also kept some of the hot dishes on the top of the stove or in the oven.

Along about three the men had all sides finished. A second row of timbers were placed on the second floor so they could start on the roof.

Zach said, "We still have a lot of food. Why don't you fellows take a break and have some more to eat. If you can get the studdings in, I can complete the roof myself."

Bill answered, "We'll work until it gets too dark to see as we want to see the completed job. We've some men at our ranches to see to the chores."

After the men had eaten the second time the women put things away, washed the dishes and cleaned the tables. The women enjoyed sitting around and talking after they had finished their work. By this time, the children were tired, and they just sat and talked with each other.

At last the men decided the job was far enough along Zach could finish up the details that were left. They gathered up their families, loaded them into the wagons and were on the way to their homes.

Zach said to all of them, "I don't know how I can ever repay you for such a fine job. Thank you so much."

"Don't worry, we always help each other. Maybe another time you can help us."

So the barn was almost finished. Zach would have to put in several more hours on the windows, doors and stalls. He went over to Mandy and held her in his arms and said, "Well, my dear, we are on our way to a beautiful ranch."

CHAPTER TWENTY-ONE

THE FINISHING TOUCH

Early Thursday morning, Zach went back to the ranch to work on the barn. He had the windows and the big door to finish. He decided to wait for Bill to help him with the roof. It was a two man job and he didn't want to be on the top of the roof while he was alone, just in case of an accident.

While Zach was out at the ranch working, Mandy decided she should make curtains for the sod house. She asked Helen, "Do you think we could ride into town? I want to get material for the curtains. I thought I'd make them up and surprise Zach the next time we go out there. Red and white checked ones would give a brightness to the room. Don't you think so?"

Helen answered, "I think that would be fun. We don't have to cook supper as we've so much left over from the party, and it has to be eaten. I'll go and tell Bill to hitch up the buggy for us. I'll gather up the children on my way."

The women were on the way to town. The children were happy for the chance to go again. They found the red and white checked material they were looking for. Mandy also found some white lace for the bedroom window. While in the store, they heard a lot of excitement in the street. Everyone went out to see what was going on. There were three big freight wagons coming down the street. Mandy exclaimed, "I'll bet that's my furniture! Let's go see."

The men on the wagons asked where they could find the Denson ranch. Of course, everyone knew where it was as they had just been out there working on the barn.

Mandy said, "I'm the one you're looking for, and we're ready to go back to the ranch. If you follow us, we'll show you the way."

The lead driver said, "Thank you. We were afraid we'd have trouble finding it as there is so much land out here and miles and miles of nothing."

Helen answered, "It isn't really that bad. It's only two miles down the road to our ranch. They don't have the house built yet, but we'll store everything at our place."

The lead driver replied, "That's good news, as we're very tired and will be glad to unload the wagons. Before we go, we want to get our rooms rented so when we come back to town we'll have a place to stay."

Helen and Mandy, in their buggy, made their way to the ranch with the freight wagons following. As they came up to the turnoff to the ranch they saw Bill riding up to meet them. "What is all this? Looks like the furniture had arrived! Zach will sure be happy to see you made it. You arrived before we expected."

The driver said, "We had a good trip, the weather was with us all the way. Freight wagons can travel faster than those with a wagon train."

"You fellows follow me and I'll show you where you can unload. As for now we'll use the barn and later we'll put the trunks and other smaller things in our loft."

The wagons were unloaded. It took a long time because they wanted to place the items that wouldn't be needed right away toward the back of the barn.

Mandy was so excited her things had finally arrived, Little Mark squealed with delight, "My wagon's here, my wagon's here! Look George, Bill, Cathy, come and see my wagon. We'll have such fun."

All of the children took turns riding in the wagon. Mandy and Helen watched from the porch. Helen said, "That'll keep them busy for a long time."

"Oh, I'm so happy, at last I feel we've finally arrived in our new home."

After finishing the unloading Bill came up to the house and said, "Do you think I should ride out and tell Zach about the arrival of the furniture?"

"Let's don't. When he comes home, we'll just take him out to the barn, telling him there is something we want to show him and watch his reaction. I think it would be fun, seeing his face when he finds out what we want to show him. I'll tell Mark so he can hide his wagon. We don't want Zach to see it when he rides in."

Mark said, "Oh, that'll be great. I'll go and put it in the barn now because we want to surprise Papa."

Mandy said to Helen, "I'd better get the material put away so Zach won't find it. Can I use your bedroom? He won't be going in there I'm sure."

"You're right. Let's put it away before he gets here."

Along about six, they heard Zach coming down the road. He looked very tired, and he headed right for the barn. Mandy yelled, "Zach, wait a minute, we want to show you something." Everyone came out to the yard and followed Zach to the barn. When he opened the door, he just stood there for a second and said, "Our furniture! It's here, so that's what you wanted to show me. How wonderful. When did it come? I didn't expect it for a week or so. Oh, Mandy, now we can move into our little house."

"Yes, the first of the week. I want to look over several things and decide which to take for now and what to leave. Isn't it wonderful? We've waited so long."

Zach gave Mandy a big hug, "Monday we'll start moving our things into the sod house. It's all ready for you and the boys. All I need to do is finish the barn roof, get our stock and start living as we planned for so long. Bill, do you think you could help me with the roof tomorrow. I don't like to do it alone, just in case?"

"Sure I'll be glad to help and I'll bring two of my men so we can finish it up sooner."

Friday morning, the men rode out to Zach's ranch. They worked most of the day and finished the job. Zach was a happy man. At last, his barn was ready for stock. Now he had to find enough feed to last the winter. As it was getting close to the middle of August, the fall rains would start in a few weeks, he needed to get the feed real soon.

Bill said, "It's a good idea to get your feed in but don't you think you'd better get the fence posts before the weather turns bad? It would take at least a week to drive up to the trees along Rush

Creek. If it starts to rain up in that area you wouldn't be able to get the wagon out even with the oxen being so strong. Have you decided to take some men with you? The work would go much faster and after you return with the posts you could arrange for the feed."

Zach thought about going after the fence posts and then he said to Bill, "That means we couldn't move next week. I wouldn't want to leave Mandy and the boys out there all alone. They wouldn't have any way to get help if they needed it. I would feel better if they were staying with you and Helen."

"I'm sure if we explain the problem she'll go along with it. I know she wouldn't want to be out there without you being with her."

The men finished their work and went back to the ranch to talk to Mandy about the necessity of Zach making the trip now before the weather got bad. After they explained it to her, she agreed to stay with Bill and Helen. Zach would leave the first of the week to get the trees for the fencing.

Mandy said, "I sure hate to have you gone for so long, but I know you have to go. The boys and I will feel much better staying where it's safe. I've a lot of things to do to get our home in order. There is shopping for supplies, getting the bedding washed, oh so many things need to be done. When you get back, I'll have our house all ready. Helen said she would help me and maybe we could move some of the furniture with Bill or some of his men to help us."

"I really don't want to go, but if I do it myself, I'll save a lot of money. We can use it to buy feed for the stock. There's so many things we need to buy. We'll have to watch our spending until we start selling the stock in the spring. Now don't you worry we'll be just fine, I still have a good reserve in the bank."

It was decided that Zach would take the oxen and wagon along with two of Bill's men and head up Rush Creek to the high country to look for trees that would make good fence posts and railings.

The men went to the barn to do the chores, Mandy said to Helen, "I hate to see him go, but it'll give me more time to fix up the sod house. He won't even know it when he returns."

"I think we'll have a lot of fun fixing it up."

CHAPTER TWENTY-TWO

THE TRIP TO THE MOUNTAINS

Zach and Mandy rode out to their ranch after church. Zach wanted some time alone with his wife. He said, "Mandy, I know how hard it's been on you, not having our own place. As you can see we're almost finished with the barn, then we can start living as a family. It has been a long time, and you've been so patient in waiting. As soon as I get back with the fencing, we'll move into our little house. In a week or so, we'll start the work on the big house. When we've the main part of the house framed and closed in, we'll take our time on the interior. Our house will be beautiful. You make the plans for the decorations, the cabinets, bookcases, and all sort of things. It'll be several months before we can move. I hope you won't mind too much."

"Oh, Zach, you've been working so hard to make a place for us, we'll wait as long as necessary. Don't worry about it we'll be just fine. Think of the years of living we'll have in our house."

They rode down the road and as they passed by the trees, Zach said, "Let's sit a spell before we go back to Bill's ranch. I just want to hold you in my arms. It'll be a long time before we can be together, all alone."

Zach and Mandy sat under the cottonwood tree for a long time, listening to the water in the creek. It was such a quiet time with the sound of the water rushing over the rocks and the breeze rippling the leaves in the tree. Zach held her in his arms and gently kissed her. His hand caressed her beautiful blonde hair. He whispered in her ear, "Wouldn't it be nice if we had a little girl with your beautiful blonde hair?" Maybe you'll think about it when we move into our big house."

He wanted to show her more of his love, but this was not the time or place. They were both so happy to be all alone. Finally, Zach raised up from the ground where they were sitting.

"We'd better get back or they'll send someone to look for us. Mandy, my loving wife, thank you for such a wonderful afternoon. It'll have to last me for a whole week."

On returning from their ride, Zach began to put the necessary things together for his long trip up to the trees. Mandy and Helen were busy preparing the food for the trip—coffee, beans, dried beef, bacon, a can of flour—enough to last the week they expected to be gone.

Bill said, "If you fellows go into Eads, you can pick up some fresh vegetables at the General Store. Eads is a good size town, almost as nice as Chivington."

On Monday morning, Zach and the two men headed up Rush Creek road. At first, the going was easy, but at the end of the road they had to travel, as the wagon trains cross open land, it would be up hill and then down into a gully with rocks and lots of sagebrush and mesquite. Zach tried to follow the creek, but that was impossible because of the rocks, and once in a while, they would find a deep hole. He decided they should follow as close to the bank as they could without getting in the water. They traveled most of the day.

Zach said, "We'd better stop here for the night and give the oxen some rest. Coming back will be even slower as we'll have a load in the wagon. Bill said, "It's about forty or fifty miles up to the timber, so we'd better get there in three days. We can cut the trees in one day and start right back. It'll take at least four days to make it back if we don't run into any trouble."

The men continued on their trip with the same amount of trouble, but the oxen were doing good as they were used to a long day. At last they began to see the trees. They were happy the long journey was at an end. There were lots of the tall pole pines. The trees were only about three or four inches around and from ten to twenty feet tall. Cutting was started right away and in a very short time they had the trees trimmed and loaded in the wagon.

Zach said to the men, "A job well done. We'll rest the balance of the day. Let's plan on an early start in the morning. Going back, we can follow our tracks and won't have to look for the right spot to drive the oxen."

At first light they were on their way. As the day progressed, it began to cloud over. Zach said, "We're in for a rain storm. We must get to higher ground as a flash flood will make the water rise fast in the creek, and we won't be able to keep the wagon from slipping into the water."

As the men headed for higher ground, it started to rain. It was slow with the load they had. The oxen had to pull very hard. Finally, the men got out of the wagon. While one of them led the oxen, the others pushed from behind. At last, Zach felt they were high enough the water wouldn't reach them. They now had to find a new road home, and it would take much longer.

Zach was upset because of the detour, but he couldn't do anything but keep going and hope the way wouldn't be too difficult. By the end of the day they were ready to make camp. The rain continued and they had a hard time keeping the fire going. Finally, they gave up and decided they would have to make it a wet camp. They ate the dried beef with no coffee to wash it down. Zach said, "At least we have plenty of water."

The next morning, they started out again, and it was slow because of the mud. The clay mud was just like cement, and every once in a while they would have to stop and clean the wheels. Late in the afternoon of the second day the sun came out and things began to dry out.

Zach said, "Let's stop and have a good lunch with some coffee! We're so late now, we might as well have a little rest."

After lunch they put out the fire and started on their way. It was a difficult trip even yet as there was no road. No one had ever been on this route before, and they had to pick their way very slowly, foot by foot. They came to a high rise and they could look down on the creek. Sure enough the creek was out of its banks, and the way they had come was under water.

Zach said, "I'm sure glad we came by the higher route."

"I wonder how far down the creek has been flooded? I hope by the time the water reached the ranch it slowed down a bit." Another day of travel, it was still a rough trip. At last they could see

Eads in the distance.

Zach said, "Let's go into town and get a meal. I'm sure getting hungry for some good cooking."

They pulled into Eads about supper time and found a restaurant near the hotel. After having such a hard time on the road, they decided to stay overnight in a good bed and get a fresh start in the morning. They found a place for the oxen and rooms for themselves. It would be only another twenty miles to the ranch.

The men pulled out at sunup and the way seemed to be smoother as many people had made the trip from Eads to Chivington. It wasn't a formal road but a well marked trail.

While the men were in the restaurant, they picked up sandwiches to eat on the road. They wanted to eat on the way so they wouldn't have to stop and make camp. As they traveled on, the trail got better and better, and at last, they found the road to the ranch. It was very late, but they were home!

Zach and the men unhitched the oxen and took them to their shed. The oxen were very tired but did manage to eat a little and they enjoyed the fresh water. The men went to the bunkhouse, and Zach slowly made his way to the house. As he approached, he saw a light go on, and there was Bill standing in the doorway. "You look like you had a rough trip. Come on, and I'll warm up some coffee for you. Let me fix you a sandwich. I know you must be hungry."

Mandy came out of the bedroom, "You're home, I was so worried when the rain came. Are you all right?"

She gave him a big hug and kiss. She just couldn't let go of him. Finally Zach said, "Mandy, I'm home, and I'm hungry. Let me eat and then you can hug me all night." That made Mandy blush, and she let go. After Zach had eaten, she said, "I hope you're not too tired to go out to the ranch first thing in the morning. I want to show you what Helen and I have done while you were gone. Oh, Zach, we missed you so much and everyone asked about you at church. We told them where you were, and they understood. We were all so worried about you when the rain came."

"It was a rough trip, and I'm glad we didn't wait any longer to go after the fencing. I feel the weather is going to be unpredictable from now on. I think we'd better get busy and plan to frame the house by next week. We can send a notice to Bob for the bulletin board in the store. Sunday we'll make the announcement after church."

The next morning, Zach hitched the oxen to the wagon to take the fencing out to his place. Mandy rode along so she could be there when Zach saw what she and Helen had done to the sod house. When they drove up close to the house, Zach could see it didn't look the same as when he left it.

"Oh, how nice everything looks. You sure have been busy while I was gone. I want to see the bedroom and what you have done in there."

When he went in, there was all of their bedroom funiture, white curtains on the windows, and the bed was made up with his favorite quilt on top.

Zach gathered her in his arms, "You have made a beautiful home for us out of the old sod house. We'll move in tomorrow, how about that?"

CHAPTER TWENTY-THREE

HOME AT LAST

Zach got up early and after breakfast he headed for the barn. Mandy asked, "Are you going to hitch up the oxen so we can take the rest of our things out to our ranch?"

"Not right now, first I must ride into town and post the notice about our house raising and look for some feed to buy for the winter. I must get the feed in before it begins raining again. I'll be back by noon and then we'll load our things."

"I'll have everything ready when you get back."

Bill was talking with Zach on the way to the barn. "I'll have a couple of horses and equipment with saddles all ready for you to take out to your place, I'll send some feed too. At least enough to last a week or two until you can buy your own. It might take a while for you to find the feed. We'd like to ride out with you and help you get settled. It's going to be lonesome without you and your family around."

"That would be good. I'll need the horses for a while. I must be on my way if I'm going to be back by noon."

While Zach was gone for the fencing, Mandy had bought all the extra things needed for the house, extra buckets to haul the water from the pumps, new broom, oil for the lamps and matches. By the time Zach returned from town Mandy had everything loaded in the wagon. Bill hitched the horses to the buggy so Helen and the children could ride along. He tied the extra horses to the back of the buggy.

At last Mandy and Zach were moving into their own home.

Mandy was so happy they could be one family again. It didn't take long to get their things unloaded. Zach and Bill took the animals down to the barn and placed them in their stalls.. While the men were working in the barn, Helen and Mandy fixed lunch. Mandy gave Helen a hug and said, "My first meal in our new home, and we can share it with our very close friends. I don't know how all of this could be done without your help and letting us stay with you for so long."

"We loved having you with us, and we'll still be able to visit each week. I'll drive out to see you in the buggy until you get one of your own, then you can come to see us."

While the women were working in the house, the children were having a good time playing in the big yard. Mark had his wagon and each of the children took turns riding while one of the others pulled. Lunch was ready. Mandy asked Mark to go down to the barn and fetch the men.

After lunch, Helen helped Mandy clean up the dishes, Helen said, "We had better get back home, we'll see you real soon."

Bill said, "I'm sure it won't be long before you'll hear about your feed. If you need any help with the hauling or unloading, be sure to let me know. It'll be a big job, and I'm sure you'll need some help."

"I'll need some help for sure. I'll let you know. Thanks for the use of your horses. I'll take good care of them. I might be riding into town in a few days, I'll stop and see you. Right now I must get the fence up around the barn so the horses can have a place to run and get some exercise."

"If I get my work done, I'll ride out and help you with the fence tomorrow."

"That would be nice, but I don't want you to let your work go. You've spent so much time with us already."

Bill, Helen and the children rode down the road to their own ranch. Mandy, Zach, and the boys all waved to them as they rode away. Zach held Mandy in his arms, "Mandy, we're here at last. Now the work begins to make this a big and successful ranch."

Zach went to the barn to get things ready to dig the post holes and all of the things he needed to do. Mandy went into the house to start on her first day of many days to come taking care of her husband and their two little boys. The children came in also as they wanted to play with the toys they hadn't seen for so long. It was like they were new. All afternoon was spent unloading the boxes of toys.

At last, it was supper time, and Mandy asked Mark to get his Papa from the barn. Baby Forrest was so tired playing he laid down on his bed and was soon fast asleep.

Supper was over and Mark was settled in his bed with Baby Forrest. Zach and Mandy retired to their room. Alone at last in their own home, Zach turned down the lamp and lay down beside her. He held Mandy in his arms rubbing her back and gently kissing her good night. At last she was lost in happy slumber.

Zach went to work digging the post holes early the next morning. Around noon, Bill came with two of his men to help. It was hard digging and he had a lot of trouble with the rocks. Zach said, "Once we get the holes dug, these rocks will help hold the posts in place."

The men worked the rest of the day digging and at last all of the posts were in. Bill said, "Nailing on the rails will be an easy job. Do you want us to help with them?"

"I don't think so as it's a simple task. Thanks for the help, it would have taken me a week just putting in the posts."

Bill and his men went back home, telling Zach if there was any more they could do, just let them know. As it was getting close to the end of the day, Zach decided to feed the animals. After he put his tools away he led each animal out to the water trough for a drink. He talked with them as he took each one out for water, "Tomorrow you fellows can get your own water as the fence will be finished."

He decided to make a small enclosure now, so the animals could get water. Later, he would make the area larger when he got more stock. At last, he made his way back to the house.

The next day, Zach finished nailing on the rails to the posts and piled rocks around each post. Later, when he had more time, he wanted to place rocks all along the fence line. He thought it would look nice and also keep the animals from jumping the fence.

When he finished the job, he let the horses out so they could run around a little. The oxen didn't want to come so he had to lead them to the water trough. After they had their fill, he let them loose to see if they would go back to the barn on their own. Sure enough they turned around and went back to their stall. As he watched them he said to himself, "I guess they would rather eat than walk around the yard."

He went back to the house and told Mandy he was going into town the next day and asked her if she wanted to go along.

"If you want to go, I'll hitch the oxen to the wagon. If not, I'll just ride one of the horses."

"I'd like to go as we need some fresh vegetables. Next year we'll have a garden and won't have to buy so much. Won't it be fun growing our own things?"

Early the next day they went to town for shopping and to check if there was any feed available. As they were riding along Zach said, "Let's have lunch at the restaurant and then you can shop. I must find out where I can get the feed. I'm sure someone will have some for sale. Bill said there is always one or more of the ranchers that raise more than they can use."

Zach went into the store and checked the bulletin board, he found several people had a notice listing feed for sale.

He was happy to know he was going to have feed for the winter. There was a list of people willing to come for the house raising.

Zach said to Bob, the store owner, "Looks like we're going to have another party. Lots of people signed up. Could you tell me where I can find the people that have the feed for sale?" Bob gave him a map showing where each of the ranches were.

He decided he'd try the ones closer in first, and if it was necessary, he'd see the others later. He thought, "I'll ride out and check the ranchers tomorrow. I can't wait too long if I want to get my starter herd before winter sets in."

Mandy and the boys were in the store to pick up the things they needed. Zach told her the good news.

Mandy said, "I think we've all the things we'll need for the party Wednesday. I'll drop you by Helen's when I come in Monday or Tuesday, how about that?"

The happy couple and their two little boys made their way back home.

When Zach rode out the next day, he found the ranch where

the feed was for sale and made arrangements to come and get it on Monday. He decided to stop by Bill's ranch and see if he could use his wagon and two of his men to help him get the feed up to the loft of the barn.

Zach dropped Mandy and the boys off at Bill's Monday morning and got the men together for the drive over to pick up the feed. After loading, they made the long trip out to Zach's ranch.

It took most of the day to unload. They decided they'd make another trip on Tuesday for the rest of the feed he had bought. The four wagon loads should be enough to get him through the winter.

The feed was in and stored and today his house would be framed. Just as before with the barn, people showed up from everywhere. The house was a difficult task, it had to be done with much more care. They worked with the specs Bill had and that made it eiaser to put the building together. They left a big space for the fireplace and also spaces for the windows and doors. Zach decided while the house was in the rough stage he'd have a stairway built to the second floor.

The work continued the rest of the day, as when working on the barn, with lunch and rest stops once in a while. It was getting on to dusk, they decided enough work for the day. Bill came up to Zach, "My men and I'll come out tomorrow and finish the roof."

"Thanks, if we could get the roof on, the interior can be done as time permits."

Zach, Mandy and the boys walked up to their house and enjoyed the view from where the living room window would be.

Mandy said, "I'm going to love sitting here and doing my work by this window, looking out over the hills and valleys."

The boys kept going up and down the stairs.

Zach said, "Be careful as there's no railing, you might fall."

This was the beginning of many happy years on their ranch.

CHAPTER TWENTY-FOUR

THE STRANGER

As the days and weeks passed, Zach continued to work around the ranch. He finished placing the rocks around the fence line. Bill's sled was still there so he used it to move the rocks around with the help of the oxen. When the rocks were done, he started to work on the main house. The roof had been finished for several weeks and the windows were ready to install. There was a lot to do because there were so many. The living/dining room had a big one in the front and one on each side of the fireplace. In the kitchen there was a long window over the cabinets and the installed sink. He made a place to put a pump on the side of the sink to be connected to the big outside pump. The downstairs bedrooms had two windows each. It was the same in the upstairs bedrooms. Zach decided that he'd finish the upstairs after they moved in, but he'd still had to install the windows.

There were two doors, one in front and another off the kitchen, both were easy to install. A big job was yet to come, building the fireplace. He decided he'd ask Bill and his men to help. He could get the rocks piled so they would be ready. Many things had to be done in finishing the inside of the house, paneling with heavy boards would be a hard job and it would take a lot of time. Making the cabinets in the kitchen would be very detailed. Zach worked several weeks on the house. One day while Mandy was preparing the noon meal, she heard a horse coming up the trail toward the house. She looked out of the open door, thinking it might be Bill. It wasn't. A stranger was riding in. He appeared tired, with his hat pulled down over his face, she couldn't see who it was. She was a little afraid. Who could it be? As the horse stopped at the rail in front of the house, the man fell off and landed in a heap at her feet. She called for Zach to come, but he was in the house working and he didn't hear her. "Mark, run and get your Papa. This man is hurt."

She pulled his hat off. She looked at his face and found he was just a boy, no more than sixteen, if that. She wondered why he was out here, so far from town.

Zach came running with Mark at his heels. "What's the matter? Who is this boy? Let's get him in the sod house and out of the sun."

Zach picked him up. He was a tall boy but very thin. It looked as he hadn't eaten in days. Mandy bathed his face with a soft cloth while Zach removed his worn boots. His feet were bare, red splotches, and sores were all over them.

"This fellow is in bad shape. Let's see if he'll come too. I can't give him water while he's still out."

Mandy took a wet rag and dabbed his lips. At last he began to move. His eyes were open. "Can I give him a sip of water now?"

Zach raised his head. He was very thirsty, but Zach gave him only a little at a time.

At last he could speak. "Where am I?"

Zach told him of his arrival and asked him who he was and why was he in such a sorry shape.

"Let's get some soup in him. He looks so hungry."

She fixed a bowl, and as he was so weak, she spooned some in his mouth. After a while he said, "I feel better. I'm Jim Reaves. I was looking for some work, but no one needs any help. I just kept on looking. I didn't have any money to buy food. I turned down your trail, when I saw the smoke from your stove ."

"You're in no shape to do any kind of work. First thing is to get some meat on your bones. We'll talk later. As of now, just lay back and rest. Finish the soup, and I'll take your horse down to the barn. He looks like he could stand some food too.

After Zach left to take care of the horse, Mandy said, "You look like you haven't had a bath for a long time. I'll heat some water, get out the big tub, and lay some of Zach's clothes out for you. You go into the bedroom and have a good wash, then you and Zach will talk about your future. Now don't worry, we'll see that you are fed and made well again. I'd like to know why you're all alone. You're much too young to be by yourself."

Jim took a long time in the tub. Mandy was worried about him. Maybe he passed out again.

When Zach came back, she asked him to check and see if he was all right. He was. He was slow getting dressed because Zach's clothes were too big for him. He was trying to figure a way to hold his pants up. Zach gave him a belt. That helped. They sat down at the table with cups of coffee.

Zach said, "Tell me young fellow, why are you on your own?"

"A few months ago I was out hunting, when I got back home the house was burned to the ground. Mamma and Papa were in the yard. They were both dead. I didn't know what to do! I buried them before I left. I didn't have clothes, money, not even a bed roll. The camping stuff was all burned or taken away. I was so upset I just left. I picked up some odd jobs here and there, but they wouldn't pay me the going rate because I was just a kid."

Zach asked, "Where did all of this happen?"

"We lived up by Julesburg, way up north near Wyoming. I just kept going south to get away from the Indians. The Cheyenne are burning and robbing all of the small ranches that live apart from the others. I was so scared. The food you gave me was the first in five days. I didn't have a canteen so couldn't carry water. When I saw the creek, I followed it till I got here. Do you think I could help around here? I need a job real bad."

"I could use some help around here, but I couldn't pay a wage until next spring, but what I'll do is to make a place for you to sleep in the barn. It's new and clean, and we'll feed you. You can help me when you're feeling stronger. By next spring, I'll pay you a wage if you earn it. You'll need some clothes and as I had planned on getting new ones you can have some of my old things. You'll have to put on some weight before they'll fit. After supper we'll see what we can fix up for you."

"Oh thank you so much. I'll be ready to work in a day or two."

"Mandy, give me a couple of old quilts. With the heat from the animals, you should have no problem keeping warm. As winter comes on we'll think of something else. Now, let's get you settled."

A few weeks passed, and one day, Bill came out to see Zach.

"That fellow up near Eads is ready to sell part of his herd. He had a notice on the bulletin board in the store. I thought you might want to ride up there and look them over. If you decide they're what you want, my men and I will help you drive them down. Looks like the fence is all finished. Been doing a lot of work on the house? I see you've a fellow helping you."

Zach told him about Jim and what bad shape he was in when he arrived. Bill said, "You're a good man, Zach, taking him in like that. I think we could round up some clothes for him at my place. There are so many of us, I'm sure we can find some boots, shirts, pants and maybe a bed roll."

"I'd like to look at that stock. I wonder if Mandy and the boys could stay at your place with Helen? I don't feel comfortable leaving her at home alone. She wouldn't have any way to get to town if necessary."

"Helen would love that."

After Zach talked with Mandy, she was happy she could spend some time with Helen. "Maybe we could go into town and see some of our new friends. What about Jim? Can he cook for himself?"

"He has been taking care of himself for several months and with some food in the house, he'll be just fine. I'll give him a list of things to do while we're away. He might like trying to be responsible for somethings."

The men decided they would ride over to Eads on Monday. The trip would take two days as it was almost twenty miles just one way. Helen drove out to Zach's ranch with the buggy to pick up Mandy and the boys. She was happy to meet Jim. She told Mandy, "I think he'll grow up to be a nice man. It's good for Zach to have some help."

Bill rode his horse so they could continue on to Eads.

Zach said, "I'm glad I got that fence in. The horses and oxen can come out of the barn anytime they want water. With Jim's help we dropped enough feed for several days. They'll be fine without me being there. Jim isn't strong enough to do any heavy work, but he will be in time."

CHAPTER TWENTY-FIVE

THE TRIP TO EADS

The men made the trip to Eads in one day and decided to stay over night and go on in the morning to look over the stock. After a good night's sleep and a hearty breakfast they rode out to the ranch to look at the stock. Zach was pleasantly surprised with the animals that were for sale. They looked real healthy with quite a bit of weight on them. Zach decided on three cows, one bull and four head of steers. He also picked out a milk cow for their use.

Zach and Bill made their way back to Chivington. On their way home, they made plans to drive the stock from Eads to Zach's ranch. It was decided they would need three men in addition to themselves to drive the stock the twenty miles. It would take at least three days to make the trip back. On the way home, plans were made on what food was needed for the trail. Bill picked three of his best drovers and a pack horse to carry their food and supplies. The women were busy putting together the food, blankets and other necessary equipment.

At last they were ready for the trip. Mandy and the boys stayed with Helen waiting for their turn. Bill sent one of his men out to Zach's ranch to help him care for the stock and do a few odd jobs around the ranch.,

The trip to Eads was easy and uneventful, and they were happy to arrive just in time for supper. After they put the horses in the stable for the night, they had a good meal in the restaurant. Early next morning, they were off to pick up their stock, nine head.

On the way back to Zach's ranch, they were blessed with good weather. It was beautiful with no threat of rain. The men were glad because if it did rain there was always a chance of lightning. It would frighten the animals and they would be hard to control.

They couldn't follow the regular trail because it wasn't wide enough for all of the stock. The men had to pick their own route, traveling up the hills and down into the valleys over and over again. By having no rain they had to face the choking dust that flew from the hooves of the animals. They fought loose rocks and sand that made the trip go slowly. All day long they drove the stock with one man on point and two of the men riding flank, one on each side of the stock. Zach rode flank with the pack horse and hoped he wouldn't have to let go of the horse to chase one of them. Two men rode drag (behind the stock). They had the dirtiest job because of the dust kicked up by the animals.

At last they came upon a flat valley with lots of grass. It was decided this would be a good place to make camp for the night. Bill said, "We'll have to take turns sleeping as the stock must be watched at all times. I suggest a two hour watch for each man. That way we'll all get some sleep."

Zach took the first watch from 8:00 to 10:00, and then he woke one of the men to take the next watch. It felt good to lay down on his blanket and stretch out his legs. Time passed. It was so peaceful and quiet he fell asleep almost at once.

He had been asleep about two hours when Bill shook him and said, "Get up. We must get the cattle moving. It has clouded over and looks like it might rain. We have to get the cattle to higher ground and stay up with them because if it does rain we might have lightning. I'm afraid we'd have our hands full keeping them from stampeding."

"It was such a beautiful night when I went to sleep. How could it get so cloudy so fast?"

"It just does that in this part of the country. The wind changes, and all of a sudden, the clouds come down from the mountains. There is a real wind tunnel coming out of the canyons in the high mountains."

"Let's get busy, we don't want the animals spooked."

All of the men were up and stored their gear on the pack horse except their slickers. They were sure they would be needed when the rain came. By the time they were ready to move on, it had started to sprinkle. The stock were moved slowly to keep them from getting excited. Up the hill, they pushed them, gently and slowly on and on. In the dark, they couldn't see the sagebrush and the mesquite shrubs. Some of the mesquite were four or five feet high. Once in a while they would run into a small tree.

Zach said to Bill, "I'm sure glad you gave me these chaps to wear, I wouldn't have anything left of my pants."

"I was sure we'd need them since we had to make our own trail. We can stop here as it's high enough, the water can't reach us. We'll have to keep riding around the herd, if there is a strike of lightning, we'll be able to hold them."

As the rain continued, a few lightning strikes made the animals jumpy, but they held them tight without any problem.

At last it was dawn, the rain slowed and then stopped altogether.

Bill said, "We've had a busy night. I feel we should rest for a few hours and let some of you get some sleep. Around noon we'll continue until dark. I hope we'll have a quiet night and get the rest we need."

The drive went on three more days. They had good luck the rest of the way. No rain and just enough wind to keep the dust blowing away from them. The men were getting tired of camp food and couldn't wait to get back to the ranch for a home cooked meal.

At last they saw the creek trail ahead. That made them hurry the stock along a little faster. When they reached Zach's ranch they turned the herd toward the barn and fenced yard.

Zach had made a separate yard for the bull because it was too early in the year to have the cows with calf. He figured early December would be soon enough, as he didn't want calves until late spring. It would be hard to care for them if they dropped while it was still cold.

Jim was glad to see them, "We did a lot of odd jobs while you were gone, but we're sure happy you're back. I'm not too good a cook, neither is this fellow."

"Tomorrow, Mandy will fix you a good meal to make up for the time you were on your own."

It was late in the afternoon when they rode into the yard a

Bill's ranch. Mandy and Helen ran out to meet them. Lots of hugs and kisses. Both of the men hugged their children and told them how much they'd missed them.

Helen said, "All of you men get cleaned up, and you can have supper with us. I know you missed home cooking."

Zach answered, "That'd be wonderful. If we could use your buggy I'll take Mandy and the boys home tonight. I want to be there in the morning to be sure the stock are all right."

After supper, Zach, Mandy, and the boys headed back to their home.

CHAPTER TWENTY-SIX

ZACH'S NEW CLOTHES

Zach was up early to check on his new stock. He was a happy man standing by the fence looking over the beginning of a very successful ranch. The rocks were placed around the foundation of the barn and the fences. A corral for the bull had been built toward the back of the barn so he could have access to the water tank. The steers had a path between the fences from their corral to the water. All of the horses, cows, and oxen were in the central corral and could go in and out of the barn whenever they wanted to eat.

Because the weather might turn bad at any time, feed troughs were in each of the corrals so that the feed would be kept off the ground.

While he was looking things over, he made a mental list of the clothes he needed. First of all, he had to get a hat with a bigger brim, a stetson was the answer. When he was on the trail with Bill and his men, he realized how necessary the hat would be. They used it to carry water for their horses, to fan the campfires into a blaze, as a pillow and most of all, a sunshade. The stetson hats were shipped all of the way from Philadelphia and were made of rabbit-skin felt. It would protect his head against cold, hail, rain, wind, and the sun. A cord under the chin would keep it from blowing away in a fast ride or wind. He'd have to order one in his size. At the same time, he'd have to order two pair of boots, one pair for work and one pair to go to town and church. The boots had to have high-heels and he also needed some spurs to make it easier for him to ride and control his horse. A couple of pair of pants made of a long wearing material, denim was the answer. He heard Levi jeans were the best for wear and tear. Chaps was the next item, a full-length leather leg covering he could wear over his trousers so he wouldn't be scratched when riding through the sagebrush and mesquite. On the way back from Eads with the cattle, he found they were a big help because of the scrub and thorny chaparral. He had the yellow slicker, that was a must. Several blue handkerchiefs, very large and cotton, were next on his list. Blue was the only color as red couldn't be used as it might frighten the stock. He would like to have silk ones, but they cost too much.

The men on the trail used their bandanas tied around their cheeks, mouth, and nose to keep out the dust. There were many other uses, such as protection against sleet, snow, and wind. Sometimes used as a face towel. The fellows said they were also used as a blindfold for a horse or calf, a bind to tie a calf's feet together, or a potholder to hold a smoking-hot branding iron. They dried their dishes and even sometimes used it as a handkerchief to wipe off the sweat.

Now for the more expensive things. He had to have a fine buggy so Mandy and the boys would have a way to get around. At times it would be necessary for her to go somewhere when he was gone. The only way would be with a buggy because of the boys. She couldn't take them on horseback. Of course he would need horses for the buggy, two would be better, he hoped he could find a matched pair and for himself a good horse and saddle for riding on the range.

The men on the drive had saddles with a horn or sometimes called a pommel, that stuck up in front of the saddle and therefore in front of the man. It could be used to hang a rope also called a twine, a lariat, or a lasso. The rope, thirty to forty feet long was of rawhide or hemp. The saddle had a cinch, a leather belt around the horse. The cinch would be tightened as a person would tighten their belt. The horse's reins usually were not joined or tied together behind the horse's neck, therefore no loop to catch on a bush or branch or entangle the rider. When the reins were dropped on the ground, a well-trained horse would stand still—and not wander. He hoped he could find such a horse.

Zach decided that was enough thinking, he'd better get back to the house for lunch and make plans to go into town.

He still had Bill's buggy, it would be nice for Mandy and the boys to go with him.

Mandy said to Zach, "Oh, we'd love to go into town and do some shopping while you're taking care of business. Let's start first thing in the morning. I've some things to take care of this afternoon and by going in the morning, we could have the whole day."

Early the following morning, Zach, Mandy, and the boys were on the road to Chivington. Zach said, "Let's stop at Bill's place and tell them we're going into town."

"That's wonderful, I'd like to see Helen and the children."

Bill and Helen were in the yard when they drove in. "Hi, looks like the family is out for a ride," Bill said.

"We're going shopping for some things we need at the ranch. I've found my old farmer clothes are not working too well. I'm going to order some proper ones. Also look for a good saddle horse, a buggy, and I hope, a pair of horses. Mandy needs some way to get around if I happen to be gone, looking over the ranch or in town."

"Sounds like you folks are going to have a busy day. I'm sure you'll find what you need. The blacksmith always seems to know where the best horses are. He also makes buggies, if he doesn't have the one you want now, he'll make you one just to order."

"I hope he'll have one I'll like. We need to get yours back to you as soon as possible. I'm sure Helen would feel better if she had transportation available to use."

Helen answered, "If necessary I can always use the buckboard, it's not as comfortable but it would get us where we need to go."

"Zach, we'd better be on our way, we've many things to see about."

"You're right, we'll see you when we get back from town. I hope we can find a buggy. If we do we'll drop yours off on the way home."

Helen asked, "Why don't you folks plan on having supper with us. That way Mandy won't have to cook tonight."

"Oh, that would be nice, but we don't want to put you out." As they drove down the road to town, Zach said, "I'll drop you and the boys off at the hotel. You can see all the people you want to from there. Who are you going to call on first ?"

"I think I'm going to see the school teacher first. I want to pick up some teaching books for Mark. He's too little to go six miles to school, so I thought I'd start him at home. When he gets a little bigger and we can find a horse for him, he can ride to school. I think it's very important to get him started as soon as possible. Then I'm going over to the store and pick up some things we need around the house. If I've time I think I'll stop by the doctor's office and get a check up for the boys and maybe pick up some medicine, just in case one of us gets a cold this winter. A person should always have home remedies around."

"You've been doing a lot of thinking too. Don't you think Mark is too young for learning? He is only five, and he has plenty of time for that. Are you going to see the doctor for the boys or for you? Are you feeling all right, you're not sick are you?"

"I'm fine. I just want to have all the necessary things in the house this winter. What if we're snowed in or you can't get into town? I'm just being prepared. As for Mark, what is he going to do all winter if he can't get out of the house? He might as well be doing something useful and it won't hurt him a bit. I won't push him if he is not ready."

"Well, if you put it that way, I guess it'll be all right. Here we are at the hotel, I'll meet you here about noon, we can have lunch in the restaurant."

Mandy and Zach met at noon and went over the events of the morning. He asked, "Did you see the teacher? What did she say about Mark starting his learning so early? How about the doctor, did you get the medicines you wanted?"

"You're full of questions. Yes, I talked with the teacher, and she thought it was a good idea, but doesn't want him to work to hard. She also said if I taught him with her books for a year or two and if he could pass the necessary tests, she would place him in the second or third grade when he can go to school."

"That sounds like a good idea if you think you can teach him at home. How about the Doctor. Did he check the boys?"

"The doctor is Ben Conover. He was out this morning on a call

THE BAR Z RANCH

but his wife, Alice, said he'd be back this afternoon. I've planned to see him later. I bought everything we need at the store except the things Doctor Ben might recommend. How was your morning?"

"The blacksmith has a buggy, but he wants to paint it and check the wheels. It has two seats so it'll be nice for the boys when they are older and can sit by themselves. It's been sitting around a long time. He has to give it a complete cleaning. As for a pair of horses for the buggy, he doesn't have any on hand like I had in mind. He said he knew a fellow that might have what I want. We can see him Sunday when we go to church. The blacksmith said that would be the first time he would see him. I found a good saddle horse we can take home with us. Her name is Patty. I'm sorry we can't take our buggy home today, but by the first of next week I hope the horses and buggy will be on our ranch. We'll have to pick up Helen and the children for Sunday School. Bill and I can ride our horses."

"How about your clothes? Did you find what you wanted?"

"I found the shirts, handkerchiefs and pants. I bought a good saddle with all the trappings, a pair of spurs and chaps. The boots and hat have to be ordered as they didn't have any in my size. It'll take two or three weeks for them to get here. I'll have to make do with the things I have now. I picked up a heavy sheep fur lined coat for the very cold days I'll be riding out on the range. Well now, I think we'd better get on with the rest of the things we've got to do. My, that was sure a good lunch. Did you enjoy eating without having to fix it?"

"It was so much fun. I feel just like a great lady. The boys had a good time in town haven't you?"

"My dear, you are a fine lady. When you're finished with your chores come back to the hotel and we'll start home from here."

Mark said, "We're having such a good time, can we do this again real soon?"

As they left the hotel, Mandy said to Mark, "I don't know when we'll be back, but I hope it's soon as I'm having a good time too. We must get over to the doctor's office and get the medicine we'll need for the long winter ahead of us. After we're all done we'll go to the store and maybe we'll find some candies, how about that?"

"Oh goody, did you hear that, Baby?"

Toward the middle of the afternoon, Mandy and the boys went

back to the hotel and there was Zach waiting for them. Mandy found that Zach did have a beautiful horse. She was tied behind the buggy for the trip to Bill's ranch.

"Did you get everything you'll need to take care of us this winter?"

"Yes, we're all fixed up for the next few months. The doctor said the boys are fine and I'm fine also. He said since I was there I might as well be checked too."

Helen had a good supper all ready for them when they got back. After much conversation and good food, Zach and Mandy headed on to their own ranch. Zach had to do chores after he got home and didn't want to be too late.

CHAPTER TWENTY-SEVEN

ZACH AND MANDY HAVE A TALK

Mandy made the boys ready for bed as soon as they got home. They were so tired after the exciting trip to town and were fast asleep as soon as they were settled in their bed.

She got busy putting away all the things she had bought while in town. "I must put the medicine up high on the top shelf so the boys can't reach it." Mandy was thinking to herself.

At last she had everything put away and set herself down in her favorite rocking chair and picked up her knitting. While she was sitting, rocking and knitting she was thinking about all the things she had heard when she was in town.

Zach came in from doing his chores and said, "All of the animals seem to be happy with their surroundings. But I don't know what to do with all of the milk we're getting from the cows. I think I'll put two of them in with the bull for a few days. We can handle new calves if we keep the cows in the warmth of the barn this winter. If they drop their calves early enough, I might be able to breed them again for a fall delivery. Looks like you have your work done for the day. It's nice to see you sitting by the fireplace with your knitting."

"Yes, everything is in the right place and the boys are asleep. They were so tired from the trip to town. Zach, get yourself a cup of coffee and let's have a talk. I heard some things in town that upset me a little. I'd like to talk to you about what I heard."

Zach came over to her chair and put his arms around her, "What is the matter, Mandy? Things are going real well, and we've a good start on our dream of a successful ranch."

"I heard the men at the hotel talking about raids on some of the ranches. Do you think the Indians might come here?"

"Don't worry, my dear, I talked with Bill after I heard the rumors. He said they hadn't had any trouble around here. Most of the raids were down south in New Mexico. Some of the troubles are in Wyoming, Minnesota, and the Dakotas. We don't have anything to steal around these parts"

"Did you know about all of this warfare when we came out here? Didn't it worry you about bringing us out to this wilderness?"

"I knew about some of the things that happened several years back but just since we've been here I heard about the guerrilla war. I didn't want to worry you so I thought it best not to say anything."

"I'm glad you didn't tell me because I'd been more concerned than ever. Do you think we need to worry about Indians now?"

Zach held her in his arms. "No, there has never been any trouble around here. I've talked with lots of the men and they all tell me the same thing. As I was talking with them they also told me they expected some surveyors from the railroad to come to town in the next few weeks. They are surveying all of the land that has been homesteaded in the last year. They are also making measurements for a rail line to come to Chivington, on to Eads and Denver. It'll be a spur line and will be used for shipping cattle or feed. I'll be glad to have our land surveyed, then I can build my markers. No one knows where our place starts or ends."

"Railroads are being built all across the land, and the Indians do not like the rails covering their land. I think that might be the reason for the trouble along some of the other lines. I don't think we'll have any trouble as this part of the country is not important to them. Union Pacific is building a line north of here through Nebraska and the Kansas Pacific is building from Kansas City to Denver. The railroad you saw in Lamar is the Atchinson, Topeka, and Santa Fe from Kansas City to Dodge City then on to Lamar. They expect to be all the way to Denver in a few months. I'm very enthusiastic about the rails because they would save us a lot of work and the animals wouldn't lose the weight they would in a long drive. Now, my dear, I think we'd better get to bed. Don't worry your pretty little head about the things of the past. We're fine and will continue to be."

Zach went over and checked the boys to see if their covers were over them. "The boys are fine and so are we. I think I'll spend some time on the house tomorrow. In a few days I'll have to make another trip to Lamar. What do you think of building a carriage house with an extra room?

It's going to be too cold for Jim in the barn this winter, and we could use the space for him or any more hands we might pick up before our house is finished. I'd like for our buggy to be inside, out of the weather and it would help keep it clean. I want to pick up some timbers to build a dug out or as Bill calls it a summer house. It would keep things cool in the summer and also keep them from freezing in the winter.

When I talked with Bill the other day, he said they would help build the fireplace but I think I had better go to Lamar before we do that. I won't go until our buggy is here, that way if you need to go somewhere Jim can help you with the horses and even drive for you until you're used to them. I must get my traveling in before long as it might blow up a storm at any time. I want to be safe at home when that happens."

Mandy and Zach retired for the night but Mandy was still thinking about the Indians.

CHAPTER TWENTY-EIGHT

PREPARING FOR WINTER

After Zach picked up his buggy and the pair of horses Monday morning, he made ready for his trip to Lamar. He planned to make the trip alone as the load wouldn't be as heavy as the materials for the sod house.

He wasn't worried about Mandy and the boys because Jim was now capable to take care of the ranch. He knew he would watch over his family as if they were his own. They had become very close in the last few weeks. Zach felt it was necessary to build the carriage house as soon as possible, it was now the middle of September and the weather might turn cold at any time. Jim needed a real room to call his own. With a pot belly stove, a nice bed, table and chairs he'd feel like a real person, not just part of the stock living in the barn.

Zach said to himself, as he made the long trip down the road, "As soon as I get back I must take Jim into town and buy him some clothes. With winter coming on, he'll need a warmer coat, some gloves and wool socks. I can pick up my hat and boots too. I'm sure they are in by now. I still can't pay him a wage but the warm clothes will help him get through the winter. The things Bill and his men gave him were good but not for the cold weather we are expecting."

Zach's four day trip was successful with no problems with the oxen or the weather. He bought enough lumber and windows for the carriage house and some timbers for shoring of the dugout.

Mandy, Jim, and the boys were all glad when he got home.

Bill and his men came out the next day and started building the carriage house. The work went well and before the day was over the frame and roof were completed. Zach thought he and Jim could finish the rest of the job themselves, but he would like some help with the dugout. Lots of rocks had to be moved while they were digging. As the work progressed further into the hill timbers were placed every four or five feet with a cross beam on each pair of timbers. The work continued for several days and at last they felt they were deep enough into the hill to make it safe for the potatoes, vegetables and any of the other things to be stored. Zach made a heavy door for the dugout to keep things from freezing in the winter and cool in the summer. Jim and Zach finished the carriage house and made a table, chairs and a bunk bed. Zach told Jim, "Tomorrow we'll go into town and do some shopping."

They made their trip to town so Zach could get some clothes for Jim, mattress for his bed and a pot belly stove for the carriage house. Jim would need one to keep his room warm. They expected lots of cold weather this winter.

As they rode back to the ranch Zach said, "Well, Jim, our big jobs are done for now and we can start acting like real ranchers."

The happy family worked each day on the improvements around the ranch. Zach decided the next project was to make storm shutters for each of the windows. He thought he would place them on the inside of the buildings so they could be shut from the inside of the house if the weather turned bad during the night.

Shutters had to be made for the sod house, the carriage house, and the main house. The barn had shutters built in at the time of the construction.

Zach and Jim were finishing up the main house, and toward the end of the day, it started to rain hard.

Zach said "Let's close all the shutters here in the main house because we don't know what will happen during the night. I'm glad we got the fuel box full of wood because it might be snowing by morning. Do you have your box full?"

"Yes, I filled it with some scraps of wood left over after we finished the building. I also picked up some mesquite that was laying around. I'll be nice and warm in my little house."

"Let's get up to the barn and secure the windows so the animals will keep warm."

"What'll we do with the bull and the steers? Will they be all right?"

"I think they'll make it tonight, but I think we should build a partial shed for them so they can get under cover when it's real cold."

Everyone was settled in for the night, expecting to find snow when they got up. But when they looked out the next morning they found sleet covered the ground and buildings. It was hard to walk up to the barn. Jim came out of his nice warm room in a hurry, as he always was, and slipped on the ice and fell on his back. He got up laughing, "This is the weirdest snow I've ever seen."

The men opened the shutters in the barn so the animals could get some air. Zach said, "Looks like the storm has moved on and the sun will be out soon. At least it didn't freeze the water in the troughs. I'm sure glad we got the shutters in place. We should get started on those sheds as soon as we feed the stock and milk the cows."

As they were working they heard horses coming down the trail. It was Bill in the buckboard. "Hi, how are you fellows doing? That was some snow we had, I brought you a surprise! We had some extra chickens and a rooster. We wanted you to have them. You'll need them for eggs and later in the spring you'll be able to have some baby chicks."

"What a nice thing to do. We'll get busy making a hen house for them in the barn so they'll keep warm. Come on down to the house for coffee. The chickens can stay in the coops for a while."

Mandy was glad to see Bill, "I'm glad you came today. I'd like you, Helen and the children to come out for lunch next Wednesday. We're going to have another birthday party. Baby will be three years old."

Baby said, "I'm three, and I'm a big boy."

Mark answered, "I'm glad Baby can talk to me now. I've waited so long for him to talk. I guess he never had anything to say before."

Bill said, "I must be going. We'll be here on Wednesday. Baby it's nice to have you talk to me."

As Bill rode down the trail, Zach and Jim went back to the barn to finish their work. He said, "I wish I had some wire to make a yard for the chickens."

"If you want, I can ride into town and bring some back. I'll take two horses and use one of them as a pack horse."

"I think you should take the buggy so you can pick up some supplies too. Why don't you plan on making the trip first thing in the morning. Be sure you pick up the mail for us.

Let's ask Mandy if she needs anything from town— potatoes, flour, etc. I'll give you a note for Bob. He can charge what you pick up and tell him I'll pay him next time I go to town. I'm sure he'll accept my authority by the way of a note for what we need."

"Let's go and have our supper. I can finish this up tomorrow."

CHAPTER TWENTY-NINE

THE FIRST SNOW

Jim came back from town with the wire fencing, the supplies Mandy wanted, and mail from Illinois. Mandy couldn't wait to read her letter from her friends, "Oh Zach, it's nice to read about the folks back home, but I'm happy with our new home and don't regret moving at all.

Everything is looking so beautiful on the ranch. It was nice of Bill to give us the chickens. I won't have to be so careful using eggs now. Mark will have a steady job gathering the eggs in the morning and at night. I think I'll give him a little pay for each egg he brings in not broken. What do you think of three cents for each dozen? Not much money but it will make him feel important."

"Mandy, I'm so glad you're happy with our ranch. When we start bringing in some cash, you'll be even happier. I'd better get to work on the yard for our chickens. I talked with Bill the other day, and he is going to loan me the use of his plow and harrow. He's got one of the new Kenwood Steel Walking plows. It was made for turf and stubble. The harrow will break up and smooth the soil for easier planting. I think I'll take all four of the oxen, work with two at a time while the other two rest."

"I'm going to work up the acreage down by the creek as there aren't too many rocks in the area. I plan on planting some winter wheat. It'll be only seven acres but with the right amount of snow and rain it might produce a good crop.

"When you get the fence done, the boys and I will walk up and take a look at the chickens. I want Mark to get used to them so he won't be afraid when he gathers the eggs."

When Zach finished the wire fence for the chickens, he took Jim with him when he went over to Bill's to pick up the plow and harrow. Jim enjoyed visiting with Bill's men in the bunkhouse. He was almost seventeen years old but in this day in time he was considered to be a man. The fellows asked him to come with them when they went to town on Saturday night. He told them he didn't have any money to spend so he'd have to say no. Zach overheard the end of the conversation and felt sorry for the boy. He decided he'd give him $10.00 for a little fun, all work with no play was hard on anyone especially if you're so young. Jim was happy to have a night out with the men, "I'll be careful and not spend it all in one night."

The next morning Zach started plowing the area by the creek. It was a heavy job as no one had ever put a plow to this land. He figured it was going to take at least a week to finish.

Jim came out with his lunch and asked if he could help, but he wasn't strong enough to hold the plow in line. Zach came back each night dead tired and went to bed right after supper. He was glad Jim could take the responsibility in feeding and caring for the animals and all of the chores that had to be done.

All of the time Zach was working in the field, Mandy was busy with her knitting. She sang as she rocked in her chair, knit pearl knit pearl on and on she worked. She had finished her white shawl and was almost through with the red sweater for Zach. Since Jim had come into their lives she had to think about a sweater for him. She hoped she'd have enough yarn.

Her housework was easy to do and by noon she was free to work with her knitting. The boys entertained each other all day long.

Zach was on his third day of plowing, and it began to cloud over. He hoped it would rain just a little to settle the dust because he hadn't used the harrow yet. If it rained too hard the furrows would be hard to level. He decided to harrow the part he had plowed before continuing with the plow. He worked as long as he could see and the rain held off for the rest of the day.

He was almost afraid to look out of the window the next morning. There was a little snow on the ground but it didn't rain. Zach sent

Jim back to town to get the seed for his wheat.

"I'm going to plant what I've finished, then continue with the rest of the acreage."

Five days later he finished the planting and decided to take it easy for a few days. "Mandy, let's plan to go into town tomorrow. I want to pay Bob for the supplies, and we can have a day to visit around. Jim, would you like to ride along? We'll have lunch in the restaurant."

Mandy decided to buy some yarn for Jim's sweater while she was in town. Mandy and the boys visited with several of the women while Zach and Jim were talking with the men in the hotel. One of the women had just got her a new washing machine. It was called *"Superba, ball bearing, Machine." You just swing it to and fro, with a small handle, it moves so easy a child could work it.*

Mandy thought, "I sure would like to have one. I'm going to ask Zach about it! He paid so much for the buggy and horses, over $70.00, maybe he won't want to pay out any more right now. We do have a handsome black buggy, the seats are padded and lined with upholstering leather, carpets on the floor and oil burning lamps on each side. The side curtains drop down to keep out the wind and weather. Oh, what nice rides we'll have in our buggy."

The family enjoyed their day and returned home to do the chores. Mandy had dinner cooking all day in the oven, and it was ready to eat when they got home. It was raining gently by the time the men finished the chores. Zach said, "This rain is just what we need for our wheat."

During the night, the wind came up, and Zach had to close the shutters as it was getting colder. "I'm afraid we'll have snow by morning"

The next morning they woke to a full snowstorm with the wind blowing the snow into large drifts. "We're going to have a problem getting to the barn. When we do get there, I think I'll string a rope from the barn to the house so we won't get lost going back and forth. I'll string one over to the outhouse too. I wouldn't want you to get lost when you take the boys out. I see Jim waving from his door. Here he comes for his breakfast!"

"Boy, it's cold! I'm glad you got this warm coat for me." It was hard getting the feed to the stock in the corrals. They had to break the ice in the water troughs several times as it would have ice on top in about two hours after they broke it up. The bull and steers stayed in their sheds. The men had to drive them to the troughs for water as they didn't want to leave their warm spot. The chickens had water buckets in the barn but they didn't freeze.

Toward the end of the day, the men felt the stock would be all right for the night. They closed the shutters in the barn and after milking the cows, they took the milk down to the dugout. This proved to be a difficult task as they kept slipping on the snow and ice. They had lost half of the milk they had when they finally got to the dugout.

The snow had built up in front of the door, and they didn't have a shovel with them. They had to pull the snow aside with their hands. At last they got the door opened and the milk stored in the milk cans with tight lids. Zach said, "I'm glad our stock are under cover. If they were out on the range, they might have had some problems. Next year we'll have to think about that happening. We should plan on driving them close to the barn next fall so we can protect them from the weather.

We could take food out to them but water is another thing because the animals won't eat snow. I'm going to have to think about providing water for them before next winter. We should've brought a shovel back to the house so we could shovel the snow away from the doors."

Jim said he'd go back to the barn and get one so they would have it in the morning.

"You do that and then we'll have our supper and some rest. We'll have another busy day tomorrow. Looks like we're ranching now!"

Mandy and the boys had stayed inside the house except when they had to make a trip to the outhouse. On one of the really bad days she decided they would use the chamber pots and let Zach empty them when he came back from the barn.

The storm lasted three days—very busy days for Zach and Jim. Everyone was so glad when the wind stopped and the snow was not as heavy. It was the wind that caused most of the trouble. Their first snow storm was over!

CHAPTER THIRTY

THE CHINOOK WIND

A few days after the big snowstorm, the sun came out shining bright. The snow began to melt, only the deep drifts remained. Zach made his way down to the creek to check the ground where the wheat seed was planted. He found that it hadn't been disturbed by the snow and that pleased him. He knew his crop was safe for now. If the seeds could germinate in a few weeks they would grow into a fine crop of wheat. The hill above the field kept the wind from blowing directly on the worked land. There were no drifts of snow in the whole area.

The animals enjoyed getting out of the barn, they ran around the corral and the chickens explored their new yard. Zach found a lot of eggs in the nests because during the storm Mark couldn't do his job, being confined in the house.

The boys put on their boots and coats and as soon as they got outside they started making a snow man. Jim helped the boys but told them not to expect it to last too long. The sun would soon melt the snow man, and they would have to wait for it to snow again to make one that would last for a while.

Zach decided they'd work on the big house. There were lots of things to take care of—the fireplace had to be finished and the railing for the stairs. When the big jobs were done, he planned to check with Mandy and to see where she wanted her china closets, bookcases, and linen closets.

Mandy had made the sketches of the house while she was confined by the storm. When Zach asked her about them, she had everything all ready for him.

"Well, I guess we're ready to go to work. While I'm working, why don't you have Jim take you into town to order that washing machine you want so bad?"

"Oh, thank you, Zach, I'm so happy. We'll stop at Bill's place and have them come tomorrow for Baby's birthday. The snow made us postpone our party last week."

Bill and Helen said they'd be happy to come. Mandy and Jim made their way to town. She ordered her washing machine and picked up some things for the party.

After they had the birthday cake, Mandy said, "Now we have a big three year old, we have to stop calling him Baby. From now on he'll be called Babe, a big boy's name."

The party went well, and everyone had a good time. They decided to go for a walk up to the big house to look around and then down to the barn.

Bill said, "You fellows sure have done good, but you need more stock."

"I know I do. Maybe early in the spring I'll check on getting more in."

Bill's family made their way back home. While Mandy was fixing supper she could hear the wind blowing. She opened the door and looked out. What she saw scared her—weeds were blowing all over the yard and up against the door and windows. Zach and Jim were in the barn. What if they can't make it back to the house? The wind felt warm. What was happening?

At last she could see the men walking against the wind trying to carry the buckets of milk. Then she saw them empty the milk on the ground. Why did they do that?

Zach said as they came in, "The milk had sand in it because of the wind. It couldn't be used."

"Why is it so warm?"

"They call this a chinook wind. It's a warm, dry wind that blows from the mountains, over the plains that stretch from the base. The moisture-laden winds from the west coast strike the lofty barriers of the Rockies and are forced to precipitate their moisture as rain or snow.

When the ranges are crossed the winds are cold and dry. They descend down the eastern slopes of the mountains and become warmer because the air is condensed, the pressure at the base of the mountains being much greater than at the summit. The winds become warm by the increased pressure dropping from 10,000 feet to 4,000 or 3,500 feet. The descending air is always warm. By the time we get up in the morning, the snow will be gone."

By morning the wind had stopped The men fed and watered the animals and milked the cows. Mark gathered the eggs and had a bucketful. He wanted to count them right away to see how much money he had made.

Mandy helped Mark count the eggs and put some aside to be used right away. She then showed him how to put the rest in a bucket with paper between each layer so they wouldn't break. With Mark and Babe she walked to the dugout to put them away for safe keeping.

"Now the wind has stopped we've got a job of gathering the weeds. We'll have to pile them in the middle of the yard and burn them. That's the only way to get rid of the weeds. Burning will do away with the seeds and keep them from making more weeds come spring. We'll also have to check the plowed field. I hope it didn't blow the wheat seeds away! Maybe the hill sheltered the field a bit."

Zach and Jim worked gathering the bushes from the house, barn, and fences. Zach said, "We'll only pile a few at a time as we don't want a big fire. Jim, get several pails of water and set them around the fire. If it gets to big we can throw some water on it. We don't want to burn anything but the weeds and bushes."

The fellows worked all day with the burning. It continued to be warm. Mandy and the boys were glad to be outdoors. It seemed to them they had been in the house forever. They went up to the big house so Mandy could make plans for moving by early spring. She wanted to measure the windows for curtains and drapes so she could make them before they moved in.

The men continued the burning for the next two days. They took the wagon down to the plowed field to pick up the weeds and bushes that had blown in after they finished the job they returned to the work on the house.

Zach decided it was time to put the three cows in with the bull. Maybe he would have calves by early spring.

As the days passed, Zach and Jim worked on the house after chores. Mark was serious with his job of egg gathering and Mandy worked on her plans for the curtains and drapes.

"Maybe Zach would let me drive over to Helen's, and then she could go with me into town. If I had any problems with the horses in town Helen could take over for me. Looks like the weather is settled for now, I should go before it changes." Zach was worried about Mandy taking the buggy, but there has to be a first time, it might as well be now. "I'll let her go but have Jim ride along, on horseback letting her drive. She needs to get the feel of the horses. When she gets to Bill's, Helen can take over and Jim can come back and help me."

It was decided, tomorrow she'd make her first drive in the buggy! It's only four miles down the road.

CHAPTER THIRTY-ONE

LIFE ON THE BAR Z

It was now the first of October. Zach and Jim continued working on the big house. They finished the paneling and were working on the railing for the stairs. This was a big job as Zach wanted the stairs to be the center attraction in his new home. He decided to make a door at the top of the stairs to keep the downstairs area warmer in the chill of winter. Grates were made in the floors of the upstairs rooms so the heat could rise to warm the bedrooms. He placed boards over the grates because they were not going to use the upstairs for a time. With the two bedrooms downstairs, they wouldn't be needed.

Zach thought he would take his time in finishing the upper level, maybe next spring or summer. The fireplace looked real nice and he had a lot of thanks to give to Bill and his men for helping build it and the hearth.

They had a few snow storms but not as bad as the first one in September. It had turned cold, and with the wind chill, it felt even colder. The men were kept busy filling the wood boxes. Most of the mesquite around close to the house had been used so the fellows had to take the wagon farther out on the prairie to get the fuel. They found some animal chips left from when the buffalo were in the area. The chips made a good fire but not as nice as the mesquite.

Mandy worked on her knitting and helped Mark with his lessons. Now it had turned so cold she put the sweaters aside and worked on mittens for the family. She and the boys needed the coverings for their hands. Both of the men had nice leather gloves to keep them warm. As she was working, she got the idea to make mittens to match the sweaters she was knitting for everyone for their Christmas gifts.

Mark worked only an hour or so on his lessons and then spent the rest of the time playing with Babe.

Mandy didn't have any trouble with the buggy and horses and went to see Helen at least once a week and sometimes she, Helen, and the children went into town for supplies and the mail. All of them attended church almost every Sunday and sometimes Jim went with them. It was fun seeing the other ranchers.

Jim had made good friends with the men that worked for Bill and would go to town with them on Saturday night.

The man that had taken the fellows money a few weeks ago could not be found anywhere. They asked the Sheriff about him, and all he would say was, "I don't think he'll be back." Then he would let out a little laugh.

They were glad he was gone. Now they could enjoy their night out. Jim had a lot to learn about poker as he had never played before. The men were kind to him at first but when Jim started to win a few games, they became more serious in their play. Jim had never had beer before, and he had to be careful because it was a long way home, and he didn't want to fall off his horse and lay on the road all night.

As the days passed, everyone became settled in the routine of ranch life. One day at lunch, Zach announced he had registered a name for the ranch.

"It will be called The Bar Z Ranch. Jim and I will make an entrance gate with our name across the top. Everyone that comes this way will know that the ranch belongs to us."

Mandy was happy with the name and decided she would put the name on the men's shirts, handkerchiefs or any other things they would be wearing.

One Sunday morning, Zach went out to do the chores. Jim was no where to be seen. "Where was that boy? I bet he stayed in town. Too much fun!" They got ready for church and made their way to Bill's ranch to see if the men knew what happened to Jim.

Joe said, "Don't worry about Jim. He was having a little trouble staying on his horse, so we had him stay with us last night. He might have a headache but otherwise he will be all right ."

Zach was relived that Jim was at Bill's. Helen insisted they stay for Sunday dinner after church. Zach said, "That would be fine but need to get back home early to do chores, Jim might still be a little under the weather."

Helen was talking with Mandy, "I'm planning a big Thanksgiving dinner with all our hands, and we want your family and Jim also to come and eat with us."

"Let me help, what would you like for me to fix? How about pies? I could make them ahead and with this cold weather they will keep for days. We can put them in the oven to heat when we sit down to eat."

"That would be fine, but I can manage. Oh well, I know how good your pies are. Go on and make them, and we can talk later with more details. I think we should make another trip to town for supplies. We never know when we'll have another storm."

Mandy said, "I'll drive over tomorrow."

Mandy had put blankets in the buggy to help keep them warm while on the road. With their warm coats and hats (she had made knitted caps for all of them) they started back to their ranch.

Zach said, "It seems to be colder. Looks like a storm is on the way. Maybe you won't be able to go tomorrow. I hope Jim will be able to help me close the shutters in the barn.

I have the cow to milk and get the food out for the stock. I'm glad we have enough fuel in the boxes to carry us through the night."

When they got home, Jim greeted them as they arrived. "I've got started on the chores. There isn't much left to do." Mark was happy Thanksgiving plans were being made as he knew Christmas would soon follow. Babe was too young to remember much about the Christmas they had last year but Mark decided he was going to tell him all about it and all the fun they would have on Christmas day.

CHAPTER THIRTY-TWO

JIM

After a hard day gathering wood, feeding the stock and all of the other things that were part of ranch life, Jim was relaxing in his room in the carriage house. It felt good to be in his own little room with the table, chair, and the warm pot belly stove going strong. He lay back on his bunk planning to read one of the dime novels he had picked up in the General store. He had them for several weeks, but there had been so much to do he didn't have time to read his books. As he was getting comfortable, the warmth of the fire made him sleepy.

He was thinking about his life now that he had found a home.

"What a lucky fellow I am! Where would I be if I hadn't followed the smoke from Mandy's stove? I'm sure I would be dead by now."

As his thoughts continued, "The fellows on Bill's ranch have become my good friends and we have a lot of fun on the Saturday nights in town. I sure had a lot to learn about life. My folks never took me to town, and I didn't know anything about the way the fellows on the ranches lived. They work hard all week, but when they got to town they sure had fun, playing poker and drinking a little beer. I didn't know what a deck of cards looked like, but they soon showed me. Teaching me about jacks, queens, kings, aces, and all the numbered cards. After a while it was easy to count up the totals in my hand. I was always good in numbers at school. Of course I didn't go to school after we came out west. My Papa said I didn't need to know any more to be a rancher. What will my future be? I guess I'll be a ranch hand at least for a few years.

Maybe someday, when I start making some money I can save and buy me a better horse and saddle.

"My horse is all right now but I want a real cutting horse, so I can work the cattle when Zach has more stock. Maybe if I work real hard and when Zach becomes a big rancher, he'll make me a foreman. I'll be making a lot higher wages then.

"When I make more money I'll save it and become a rancher and have my own spread! Then I can get married and have the children I've always wanted around me. I sure like to be with Mark and Babe. I'll teach them to ride and rope and all the things fellows like to do. I'm sure thinking in the far off future. Oh well, a fellow has to have a plan or he won't get anywhere!

"This will be a long winter. I must work hard for Zach, he has been so good to me. He bought all those warm cloths, fed me, built me a house to stay in. Not many men would go to all that trouble. Mandy's been good to me too. She is so young to take so much responsibility or at least she looks young. Most of the ranchers' wives look so old. Maybe she hasn't been on the ranch that long. The way Zach takes care of her, she will always look like a lady. She is sure a good cook. I think I've gained twenty pounds since I've been here.

"I must build up my strength. I couldn't help Zach with the plowing because I couldn't hold the plow in a straight line I'll do pushups each morning and run several laps around the yard to make me stronger. I'll be seventeen next spring. Should I tell Mandy? If I don't tell her and she found out someway she'd be mad at me. I guess I'll tell them at Christmas time, then they'd know, maybe they'll forget by spring.

"I miss my Mamma and Papa. When I think about them I wonder if they suffered much before they were killed. They were good, hard working people. We didn't have much, but Mamma always fixed good meals. Why were the Indians so mean? We never did anything to them. We just worked our stock and had a little garden for vegetables. Mamma always had flowers growing close to the house. Since the stock were all gone, I guess that was what they wanted, but why did they have to kill my family? I wonder what they did with the chickens? They couldn't drive them away like the stock. Why did they burn the house and barn? I was so afraid! I didn't look around much, maybe the chickens were still there. I guess they can take care of themselves.

"We had only been on our ranch two years, coming from Kentucky. Mamma didn't want to come, but Papa said we'd be all right. I sure wish we'd stayed there. Maybe my parents would still be alive."

Jim turned down the lamp, he couldn't do any reading tonight. Sunday afternoon he wouldn't have to work until time to do chores. Maybe be could find time to read then. Jim went to sleep with a smile on his face. He was dreaming of a wonderful future and all of the things he was going to do with his life. He was thinking someday he'd go back to his old ranch and see if his Mamma's and Papa's graves were still there and put up a marker of some kind. That was something he felt he had to do.

CHAPTER THIRTY-THREE

THE SURVEYORS

Mandy had to wait for her trip to town because the next morning snow covered the yard. Zach and Jim were working with the stock. The cows had been with the bull for a week. They decided it was time to put them back in the barn. The chickens were doing a good job laying eggs and scratching about for imaginary bugs in the yard.

Mandy and the boys were busy with their own projects. Mandy had completed all but two of the sweaters she was knitting for Christmas presents. She was disappointed that she couldn't go into town because of the snow. There were so many things she needed, supplies for Thanksgiving and shopping for the toys she planned to get for the children for Christmas. She remembered how attracted the boys were to the hand carved wooden toys. She didn't want to wait too long as they might be sold out by Christmas. She had written to her friends and wanted to get the letters in the mail. It would take several weeks for them to get to Springfield, Ill. The snow finally stopped and the sun came out but it was still very cold. As she set in her rocking chair enjoying the warmth coming from the fireplace, she heard a horse and buggy pull up in front of the house. When she looked out, it was Bill, Helen, and the children. What a surprise!

"Hello, what brings you out in this cold weather?"

Helen answered, "It's not too bad. We wrapped up good. Bill wanted to see Zach, so we decided to ride along."

"Come in, the boys will be so glad to have you here."

Bill went on to the barn. "Hi, Zach, how's everything going? Looks like you have things well in hand"

"What brings you out in the cold?"

"Well, I wanted to ask you something without Mandy and the boys close by. Angel has had her puppies, and we wanted to give two of them to the boys for Christmas, but we wanted to be sure it was all right with you first."

"Oh, that'll be a nice surprise, and it's fine with me and I'm sure Mandy would agree. Do you want to surprise her too? I won't say anything about it."

"I think it will be dry enough for the women to go into town tomorrow, so if Mandy can come down to our place, she and Helen can go on from there ."

"I still worry about her driving in the snow, I think I'll go along. I'll have a visit with you and the men while the women make the trip to town. Helen has had more experience with the horses and it's only two miles from your place."

The women and children had a good time in town. They got all the things needed for Thanksgiving dinner. Mandy asked Helen to take the children over to the restaurant and get them started on their lunch. "It takes them longer to eat and I want to pick up their toys for Christmas without them tagging along! I'll be there in a short time."

"My, you do things early. This Christmas I want you folks to come to our place. Next year you'll be in your new home, and we can come to you."

While having lunch, they found out the surveyors from the government were in town. They had been working out of Lamar and had now reached the halfway point. Chivington would be the headquarters for this section of land. It would take several months to finish the work in this area. Later they would move on to Eads as a base.

Mandy and Helen hurried back to the ranch with the exciting news. Zach and Bill were happy to hear about the survey. They had been waiting a long time for the news. With their land surveyed, they would know where the new railway would be and they could finish the plans for their ranches.

Bill had been talking with some fellows the last time he was in town. They figured the rails would run on the south side of Rush Creek to the end of the road, cross the creek at that point and on to Eads. By using that route they wouldn't have to do much grading.

Zach said, "Now I can get my cairns up. It will take Jim and I the rest of the winter to build them. We'll need one every mile or so."

Mandy asked, "What is a cairn?"

"It's a pile of stones heaped together to form a landmark."

Later, when we can build the fences, we won't have trouble finding the boundary of our land. Bill, you said something about plowing an area around the house and barn six or eight feet wide. Why should we do that?"

"In the summer there is always a chance of a prairie fire. The plowed area would keep the fire from reaching your buildings. Winter is the best time to do it as by spring you'll have too much to do. It's best to get it done soon because the ground will freeze in the next month or so and it'll be too hard to plow. Once it's done it'll last a year or two, we did ours last fall."

"Mandy, we'd better get home. I'll have to make out a work plan with Jim."

It was cold as they made their way back to the Bar Z ranch. Mandy was glad she had extra blankets in the buggy. Each boy was wrapped in one and she and Zach shared one in the front seat.

Jim had the chores started and said it wouldn't take long to finish. Mandy was singing to herself as she put the supplies away. She decided to put the Christmas things under their bed in the bedroom so the boys wouldn't find them.

The men were glad to get back to the warmth of the house and a hot supper. They set around the fireplace enjoying the cups of hot chocolate Mandy had for all and talked into the evening about the work plans for the rest of the winter.

CHAPTER THIRTY-FOUR

THE PLOWING

Zach and Jim were out in the freezing cold of the early morning to check the area to be plowed. As they walked around the ground about a hundred yards back of the barn, they found lots of sagebrush and mesquite. Zach decided they would have to bring the wagon out and haul the mesquite closer to the house to be used for fuel. When that job was done, they would have to haul the sagebrush to the middle of the yard to be burned. After the hauling was done they could start on breaking ground. This would be a big job because of the many rocks in the area. As the plow broke ground, one of them would have to pick up the rocks and throw them aside. Some of the rocks would be too large to be moved, so they would plow around them.

Zach said, "Well, Jim, let's get to it. I'm sure it'll take a long time to go around the barn and house, it won't do itself. "

"I'm sure glad I'm a lot stronger now than I was a few months ago. I couldn't have helped much then. How am I ever going to repay you for my life?"

"You don't know how much we enjoyed having you around. You were a blessing to us. God wanted you to find us. We needed you as much as you needed us."

The men worked until time for the noon meal. As they made their way back to the house they saw a horse coming up the trail. It was Joe, Bill's foreman.

"Hi, Bill wanted me to ride out with your mail and tell Mandy her washing machine is here."

"Thank you, Joe, Mandy will be excited to get the news. Let's go in and tell her. We just stopped to eat. Why don't you join us?"

"Fine, if it's not too much trouble. Bill also wanted me to tell you we'll pick the machine up for you. He knew you're busy with the plowing."

"Thank you, Joe, it's sure a big job."

"I'd better get back. Tomorrow we'll get the machine to you and stay a while to help."

Joe rode on down the trail, and the men went back to their plowing. Mandy was so happy about her washing machine. Now where was she going to put it?

"I guess we can store it in the bedroom and roll it out to the kitchen area when I do the wash. I'm sure glad Zach put the clothes line close to the house. The breeze dries the cloths fast except when they freeze to the line."

The work continued on the fire break for several days and with Bill's men helping it went even faster. Zach was glad when it was finished.

"Tomorrow we'll burn the sagebrush in the yard just like we did the weeds a few weeks back."

Zach rode down toward the creek area to check on the wheat field. There were signs the seeds had started to grow. He was sure he would have a good crop of winter wheat come spring. The next day, Zach and Jim turned the sagebrush in the yard.

Even though it was a big fire they had no problems because the wind was calm. The boys enjoyed watching the fire from the house as Mandy wouldn't let them get too close. She didn't want to take a chance they might get hurt.

The outside work was in good shape so Zach went back to work on the big house. Jim helped him with a lot of the things but the special detail he wanted to do himself. When the wood work was finished he would send Jim into town for some varnish to complete the work. If things went as he planned they could move into the big house after the first of the year.

As the weeks went by, Jim had his Saturday nights in town with the boys. Long nights of poker and drinking. Sometimes he would stay at Bill's place for the night, then go back to the Bar Z in time to do morning chores. The men hadn't seen the stranger that took their money a few weeks back. There were new fellows from the survey team, but they were just like them, just out for fun.

Zach, Mandy, and the boys made it to church almost every Sunday except when it was too stormy.

Thanksgiving dinner was a great success. It was nice to set back and relax for the day. All of Bill's men and Jim had dinner with them.

Hank said, "That's the best food I've had in a long time. Sure beats bunkhouse grub!"

It had started to snow by the time they were ready to start home.

"Zach said, "Looks like a big one this time. I'm sure glad we got the plowing done and all the animals can be put under cover. We have a good pile of wood on hand that'll keep us nice an warm and a good supply of food in the dugout. We won't get hungry."

As soon as they returned from Bill's, Zach decided he would put the ropes from the house to the barn, the carriage house, and the dugout as he did before in the last snow. If it snowed hard and the wind kept blowing there were sure to be drifts.

With the ropes to hang on to they wouldn't wander off and get lost in the snow.

Mark asked, "What will the chickens do if they don't see me in the morning? I go for eggs everyday. I'll tell them they'll have to do without me until the snow stops."

CHAPTER THIRTY-FIVE

THE SNOW COMES

The next morning they witnessed the throws of a full blizzard. Snow drifts were up to the sills of the windows already and it was still snowing. The force of the wind made the snow swirl up and then down, then up again. Zach was glad he had strung the ropes between the buildings. The wind tore across the hills and valleys like a train trying to outrun the snow. It was cozy in the sod house. The smell of bacon and coffee made a person feel warm and comfortable.

When Zach finally got to the barn he could feel the full force of the wind. It took both him and Jim to hold the barn door as they tried to get inside. Feeding the cows, horses, and oxen was no problem as they were all inside the barn.

Getting the feed to the steers and the bull in the corral proved to be difficult. The men had to pitch the feed out of the loft of the barn and carry it to the feed troughs. The wind was blowing so hard they would lose half of each forkful they carried.

It took a long time to finish the feeding. Next thing was to get the animals to the water trough. They didn't want to leave the warmth of the barn so the men had to lead each one out. The ice had to be broken on the water trough before the animals could drink. About one half of an inch had formed over night.

After finishing the milking they carried the milk to the dugout. One of them would carry the milk buckets and the other one would break a path in the snow for him. It took two trips in the wind and snow to get the milk safely stored in the dugout. They had no trouble carrying the buckets of eggs as they didn't fall out of the bucket with each step.

The steers and the bull kept their backs to the wind with their heads down in the feed. After they finished eating they backed up against the barn to break the force of the wind. With each breath icicles formed around their noses.

Zach and Jim were cold after being outside for so long.

They headed for the warmth of the house for a hot cup of coffee. Zach said, "I hope this won't last long. We had to work real hard this morning. Next year it'll be even harder when we have more stock. We'll need more men come next winter.

The two of us can't handle the stock when they are out on the range. The feed will have to be taken to them by wagon."

Zach and Jim started early on evening chores as it would take longer than normal. The snow and wind continued for three days. Some of the drifts were fifteen feet high against the barn. The house was protected by the hill so the drifts weren't as high around the house and outhouse. All the men could do was to take care of the animals. Every two hours they had to break the ice in the water trough so the water would be available for the stock. The chickens enjoyed the warmth of the barn and had no intention of going out to the yard.

The sun came up bright on the morning of the fourth day.

Everyone was happy to be able to get out of the house. Mark, even though he was only five, wanted to shovel the snow to make a path to the outhouse and out to the horse rail in front of the house, just in case someone would come to visit. Babe played in the snow but was no help to Mark as being only three he thought that knocking the piles down was the thing to do.

Mandy had to put a stop to that as Mark was becoming very upset after working so hard on his paths.

Zach harnessed the oxen to the sled so he could drag a path from the barn to the house and on down to the road. With the drifts so high a person couldn't get to the road. While he was working, he decided the next project would be to make a road from the house to the existing road by the creek. This would have to wait till spring as he couldn't do much until the snow melted. The brush and rocks had to be cleared to make it even and smooth. It warmed during the day and the snow started to melt but long about five in the evening it would freeze again. The flattened snow became very slick and hard to walk on. By hanging on to the ropes they could walk down to the barn. Each day the sun would come out and a little more of the snow would melt away. The high drifts remained and would for some time.

As the hard work in the barn slowed a bit, Zach wanted to get back to work on the big house. Mandy asked him if he could make a little porch in front of the sod house first. She said it would help keep the mud and dirt from tracking into the house. Later when it got warmer she thought she could do her washing on the porch and keep the mess out of her kitchen.

The days passed into weeks, and soon it was Christmas time. Mandy had finished all of the sweaters and mittens. The presents were wrapped in scraps of material she found in the trunk they had shipped from their home in Illinois. She tied each one with the yarn left over from her knitting.

Mark told his little brother about Christmas, the story of Baby Jesus and the reason everyone gave each other gifts.

It would be a big birthday party for Baby Jesus. Babe wanted to know why Baby Jesus didn't come to see them. At that point Mark asked his Mother to explain this to Babe as he didn't know how to answer the question.

Babe was excited that everyone would get presents because it was somebody's birthday. "Why don't we do this every time someone has a birthday? We'd have presents all the time!"

Mandy explained that Baby Jesus was a very special person and we only do that for special people. He still wasn't sure about it but decided that his Mother knew it was all right.

Mark and Babe talked about Christmas and they decided that they would do something special for their Mama and Papa.

"I know, we'll make special pictures for them. We have paper and pencils, let's draw a picture of our house and barn with people in it!" Mark showed Babe how to draw, it wasn't very good but Babe thought it was all right.

"Now Babe, this will be a secret so don't tell them what we are doing!"

CHAPTER THIRTY-SIX

CHRISTMAS

A week had passed with no snow. The nights remained cold, but the days were bathed in sunshine. Huge snow drifts were still evident around the barn and fences. The path Zach had made from the barn to the house with the sled was almost void of snow but remained muddy during the day time because of the runoff from the snow drifts.

Mandy had been to see Helen several times planning the Christmas events. There were no turkeys or ducks to be had they decided on a big beef roast, large enough to serve all.

All of Bill's men who worked for him were invited along with Zach, Mandy, Jim, and the boys for the Christmas dinner.

The women planned for the vegetables, bread, and pies that were expected. Everyone expressed their preference. It took a lot of preparation to keep everyone happy.

A week before Christmas Zach rode out in search of a large mesquite bush. He wanted to trim it just so to make it look like a tree. Mandy worked on bows made of yarn, ribbons, and material she had saved over the years. The boys tried to help, but their little fingers couldn't hold the bows tight enough for them to stay together.

Christmas Eve Zach, Mandy, Jim, and the boys climbed in the buggy to make the six mile trip into town for the church service. It was still very cold, so they wrapped themselves in blankets. As they drove by Bill's ranch, Bill and his family pulled onto the road. As the group made their way to town, others joined them.

The candle light service left them with a feeling of comfort and inspiration. As they prepared to leave the church, it started to snow lightly.

Mandy said, "This night is so wonderful with the snow lightly falling and all our friends around us. The world is being cleansed with the snow, and our minds and bodies are as clean as the snow around us.

Helen answered with the same feeling, "It sure is a beautiful night. We had better be on our way and get these children to bed. Tomorrow is going to be a busy day. We'll see you as soon as you finish the morning chores."

"We'll be there with the food we have at our place along with our gifts."

Zach drove into their yard and helped Mandy put the sleepy boys to bed.

"I'll take a lantern and check to see if everything is shut down in the barn. The horses need to be fed after their long trip to town."

Christmas morning was bright, clear, and cold. The new snow sparkled like diamonds on the far hills as the sun began to come over the horizon. Zach and Jim hurried with the chores so they all could drive to Bill's for the Christmas party and dinner.

As they drove up to Bill's house, they could see through the big window in the front room. There stood a large mesquite bush all covered with ribbons and colored papers strung together in large loops.

Everyone was pleased with their gifts. The sweaters Mandy made fit all and the children spent a long time playing with the new wooden toys. Helen had made shirts for all the men, even Jim. She presented Mandy a hand embroidered apron.

After the women had washed the dishes and put the left over food away, Bill said to Zach, "I think we need to go out to the barn and get something."

Everyone wondered why they needed to go just now, but they didn't say anything. The men came back in a short time with two little black puppies in their arms. They gave one to Mark and the other one was put on Babe's lap. Such squeals was heard from each boy.

Mark said, "Are these for us? This is the best Christmas present ever."

Mandy was surprised also as she didn't know anything about the puppies. "Well, I guess we will have our hands full taking care of these little ones."

When the excitement died down, Zach announced that their house was ready to move into. This was his present to Mandy.

"If the weather remains clear, we can move into our big house next week and begin to start life in our new home."

Mandy threw her arms around Zach and cried, "Oh Zach, I am so happy. You didn't tell me you had finished the work on the house. You kept it a secret just for Christmas!"

Bill said, "We'll all help with the move. Let's set up the stove first so the ladies could have a hot meal for us. It will be cold in the house, we'll need to build a fire in the fireplace also to warm the rooms.

Zach replied, "Thanks for your offer to help, I'm sure we can use all the men you can spare. Now we had better bundle up our big family and head for home."

Jim held one of the puppies as Babe couldn't seem to hold him still. Mark did all right with the other one.

Mandy wished all a good night, "What a wonderful Christmas we have had. Thank you so very much."

The weather remained clear all week making for an easy move. New Year's Day found Zach, Mandy, the boys, and the puppies all settled in their new home.

Mandy said, "At last, we have a beautiful new home. We can start planning our future from this day on."

THE BAR Z RANCH
PART TWO

CHAPTER THIRTY-SEVEN

LIFE CONTINUES

January, 1871 finds Zach and his family well settled in their home. Mandy and the boys were busy unloading boxes and barrels. The weather remained cold but Zach had built a tight house so it was nice and comfortable inside. Zach made a trip into town after chores at least every week for supplies and mail.

He found the surveyors for the railway were making good progress and they hoped construction would be on the way by early spring. Zach met a new man named Ezra Cooper known as "Coop." He came from the east to Chivington bringing with him a printing press. Since a weekly paper would not bring enough income to support him, Bob Allen hired him to work in the store.

Bob found his business was growing each month because of all the new people moving into the area. Due to the increased activity in Chivington, it was decided to have an election to elect a mayor and town council. This brought lots of excitement to the community around Chivington. The event gave "Coop" his first story. Each week more and more interesting things came to his attention. He followed the work of the surveyors and the progress of the railroad. This was the first time the people got the local news in print.

Many of the young ladies around and about were excited about the handsome new fellow in town. One of the largest ranchers in the area decided that a barn dance and social would help the inactivity of the winter months. He invited all the ranchers and townspeople, with their families, together for a night of dancing and eating.

After the town council came together for their first meeting, they voted on building a Grange Hall in town. When the news was announced everyone volunteered to help with the building. Each rancher put up a little money to buy the lumber.

On completion, the Grange (City Hall) became the center of activity for the town. All occasions for socializing were cherished, from quilting bees to box socials. When it was cold enough to have ice available, ice cream parties with a cake walk were held in the Grange. Many a romance blossomed from the Saturday night dances. With so many new men working on the railway, the young ladies found a variety to pick from for a possible husband. The town, as a whole, enjoyed a happy winter even with the cold and frequent snow and wind storms.

Many games were devised to help the young single people to meet. Young women might make a man's tie from the same fabric as their gingham or calico dress. The ties would be put in a barrel and the blindfolded men would pick a tie. Those whose ties and dresses matched would be dates for the evening. Some of the ranchers would build an ice house to store the winter ice. They were made of large timbers and placed in a hill side so that no heat could enter. A heavy door was placed at the entrance.

One day when Zach was on the way into town he noticed Rush Creek was running low on water. He talked it over with Bill and they decided to ride up the Creek to see what was causing the trouble. Just as they had suspected—a beaver dam was blocking the flow. They broke up three fourths of the dam so the water could run free. They left part of the dam so the beavers would still have a home. This job had to be done every few months as the beavers would rebuild each time.

As the year moved forward Zach bought several more head of stock here and there. The ranch was shaping into a beautiful place. His wheat crop did well with the winter snows and he was sure they would have a lot of feed for the following winter. Zach decided to plant alfalfa as soon as he harvested the wheat. He hoped they would have enough summer rain to make the crop grow well.

Zach had Howard dig another well farther out on the range. With Jim's help they transferred one of the water tanks to the sight. They spent many days building the cairns and placing some pink salt licks nearby.

All during the winter months, Mandy and the boys worked with the puppies so that they would be house broken. At a certain time each day, the boys would take the puppies out for a walk. Zach found a light weight rope to attach to each animal so they couldn't get away. He said they would be able to be out by themselves by spring and have the run of the ranch.

Mark named his puppy Peter (Pete), and they named the other Paul (Paulie). Each soon learned their name and came running when the boys called. Mark continued his learning with his mother. He seemed to enjoy books and learning to write his words.

Mandy was busy with the boys and cooking for the men. She still had some time for herself. In the trunks she had shipped from their home in Illinois, she found scraps of materials left over from her sewing before they moved to Colorado.

She started piecing together a quilt. Some of the scraps were of light weight and some heavy. She sorted them into different piles so the quilt would be of the same weight throughout.

When Zach came in from a hard day on the range, he would find her busy with her sewing. He was pleased that Mandy seemed so contented.

CHAPTER THIRTY-EIGHT

WINTER IN COLORADO

All through the winter months, Zach and Jim had to ride out to break up the ice in the water troughs. Ever other day or so they would take a wagon load of feed to the stock roaming the ranch. If they were late with the feed, the stock would drift down, trying to get back to the home ranch.

The men had to dress warmly as the wind would blow the grass free of snow and tear across the exposed plains. The harshness of Colorado can cut you like a knife. The snow would come, then the wind picked up, and drifts would be made to fifteen foot depths around the barn, house, or anything else that would stop the snow. The cattle were scattered all over, caught in the drifts. The men worked for days to get the cattle out and fed.

Feeding the cattle from the back of the wagon piled high with hay proved difficult. It was hard to keep balanced on the edge of the wagon as it bumped over the snow-drifted pasture. The cows would surge around the wagon, their breath steaming in the freezing air as they bawled and pushed with a frenzy.

The blizzard was a storm peculiar only to the open plains. It was less a snowstorm than an ice-dust windstorm which drove a smother of pulverized ice into the air from the ground and carried with it a veritable cloud of icy particles which beat with such stinging cold that neither man nor beast could stand to face it.

Every few weeks a chinook wind would come and send the temperatures up forty or fifty degrees in an hour, baring the grass so the cattle could graze in midwinter. The chinook had a vicious side also. The melted snow refreezes and creates a crust that encases the grass and cuts the cow's feet.

The ranchers had another problem when the winters were cold and long—coyotes. The coyotes would wander down from the hills looking for food. They killed the calfs and cattle often close to the ranch house. Chickens or anything else they could find would do for a meal. They hunted mostly at night. Even then a person had to be on watch whenever they were out. When they found a kill had been made, the men tracked the coyote by the blood stained tracks left in the snow. At times they found the guilty one and shot it. The coyotes were clever and hard to find because there were many places to hide.

Year old calves were less vulnerable to the snow and cold weather than the newborns. The blizzards could still kill cows, suffocating them under snowdrifts before the rancher could reach them with food and water. They tried to breed their cows so the calves would arrive after the heavy snows. They figured a late calf was better than one frozen to death.

Zach kept the prize bull and the breeding cows in a shed behind the barn when the weather was bad. He wanted to be sure they were safe for breeding.

The winter was long and hard but almost every week, the family would make it to church on Sunday. Once a month they would have a Saturday night at the Grange Hall. Mandy and the boys looked forward to the parties.

When the Grange Hall was built, a room was set aside as a nursery for the small children. The women would take turns watching them while the rest enjoyed the party. The children usually slept most of the evening.

Jim came with the family for the nights at the Grange Hall. He was not comfortable around the young women, so he headed to the saloon for a game of poker with some of the other cowboys that felt the same way about women.

Thus progressed the long winters. Everyone dreamed of an early spring so they could warm up a little.

CHAPTER THIRTY-NINE

SPRING AND SUMMER

very family needed a garden. Raising one was a mean task since the wild animals competed with the ranchers for the vegetables. Rain barrels were a must to store water for the gardens.

Zach plowed a space by the house for their garden. He located it so the drainage from the well would flow toward the garden area. The men dug ditches from the well to the garden so every time water would overflow the garden would receive the moisture. He installed a rail fence around the plowed area. This would discourage the animals from invading and eating the garden.

John Deere invented a self-cleaning steel plow saving considerable toil as it cut through the tough sod more effectively without dulling the blade. In 1870, a reaper-binder machine was introduced. The reaper was very expensive so the ranchers would share in its use for a fee, thus helping the owner pay for the machine. In the spring, Zach picked up his branding iron to identify the ranch name of the Bar Z. It was time to brand his stock in case some would drift away.

Branding the stock proved to be a big job. He hired some of Bill's men to help as he was inexperienced and also he and Jim needed more muscle than they could provide. One of the men, sometimes two would do the cutting and roping, dragging, and wrestling the calves through the wild assembly line of inoculation, ear tags, branding, castration and dehorning.

This would identify and protect the cattle and determine their destiny. Some for breeding, or others for slaughter.

The men would be covered with blood, sweat and manure. After the branding the men would drive the cows toward their calves for "Mothering-up."

The men Zach hired were experienced "cowboys." Each week they would pack enough supplies for several days ride. They would start on their circle. The circle is the cowboy's name for a day's work. It often lasted several days. It might be a square, it might be oblong, or straight out and straight back. The town of Chivington continued to grow. It drew roving carnivals and medicine shows. This provided a respite from the daily drudgery of ranching.

Local and county fairs featured plowing contests, shooting and running matches, horse races, and many other events. The women's competition revolved around baking and cooking. The ranchers ate their own preserves—for instance, tomatoes preserved in brine. Hunting provided some variety in diet, as sage hen, quail, and rabbits were plentiful, and occasionally a deer or antelope. By the time of the rancher, the buffalo were long gone from these parts. The health of the people was basically good, for in their isolation, contagious diseases affected only a few.

In the spring and summer, there was the threat of hail, nature's effort to humble the work of the men. Often piling knee-deep, marble-size hailstones could crash through crops, pulverizing them to dust. Larger hailstones could cripple or kill. After the hail storm the garden had to be replanted. In some years it had to be replanted twice or three times. They always hoped the planting would not be to late for a harvest. A late fall would help for a good harvest. The alfalfa would come up again from the roots. Other storm clouds (sometimes the same ones) brought twisters blowing out of the southwest roaring like a locomotive. Their funnels of dirt and death cut improbable swathes through one ranch while leaving a neighbor's land untouched. All of the ranchers had a storm cellar, sometimes called a Summer House. The cool cellars were also used to store food and milk.

The only way to live with such unnatural natural phenomena was to joke about them. Coop printed in his weekly newspaper, "Those of us who have lost their domestic animals and fowl need not be alarmed as the chances are that such stock will be blown back by the next wind."

The extreme heat in the summer (shimmering 110 degrees.) sometimes with no wind and the unremitting sun leathered men's skin into a tough parchment. The men had crow's feet wrinkles caused by constantly squinted eyes. The women protected themselves with long sleeves, long skirts, and sun bonnets.

When the sun was hot and water ran low in the creek, they were often visited by a few Indians from the north land. By and large, they were no threat to the rancher. Mostly they came on occasional unannounced visits looking for handouts. They might steal a horse or two if the possibility presented itself.

Mandy was always afraid of them coming while the men were away. She was always looking out of the windows, checking the land. If she saw anything she did not know or understand, she and the boys would stay in the house, trusting they would go away if they didn't see anyone. Sometimes she was in the garden or looking after the chickens. Mandy had several setting hens that produced a large bunch of baby chicks. The Indians would slip up on her when she was busy with her work. She would offer them a chicken or some food from the house. They always went away after receiving the food and watering their horses.

When summer finally came, Mandy and the boys let the puppies have the run of the yard. They were now over six months old and could hardly be called "puppies." Mark and Babe both liked to help in the garden. Sometimes Babe would do a little more than pull the weeds, a carrot or turnip would be uprooted by mistake.

So went life on the range. It was a hard life but Zach and Mandy were developing a successful ranch. They looked forward to a big pay back from the cattle sale in the fall.

CHAPTER FORTY

THINGS TO COME

As the ranchers enlarged their herds, more and more freelanced cowboys came to the area. A real cowboy was always able to find work. They considered themselves, "Kings of The Range." The cowboys were lean horsemen who rode the range for long, lonely weeks. When they had a chance to ride into a town, they drank and gambled with carefree exuberance and often caused trouble. Sheriff Mike had to hire extra deputies to take care of the "boys." When a cowboy is working the cattle, there are lots of times that he needs to tie his horse where there is nothing to tie him to. He had to be able to go away and leave him sometimes for hours, and find him right there when he comes back. Some horses learn to stand ground-ties after they've jerked their mouths a few times by stepping on a hanging rein. Prices were good in 1870, 71, and 72. Zach, Bill and all of the ranchers were making the success of ranching they had planned. In 1873, prices dropped and the ranchers held their cattle from market hoping the price would rise. This made a hardship as the herds had to be fed through the winter. They were glad the rail line was completed. Feed had to be bought many miles away, as far as Kansas and Wyoming.

Zach and many of the other ranchers had the foresight to put some of their profits of previous years away so they had no problem covering the expense of buying feed.

A great prairie fire engulfed the area during the long hot summer of 1873. As they looked toward the distant hills, across the arch of the western sky, a pall of brown smoke drifted heavily down into the valley. A prairie fire could scarcely make headway on the land as denuded as theirs. The cattle were trotting eastward like a vast army in full retreat.

The galloping infernos raced ahead of the wind faster than man or beast could flee. Towering walls of orange flame and bitter blue smoke fried and choked everything they overran. They cast their eyes over the brush and debris of the open country, brush that now fanned the fingers of flame, the sagebrush massed in the bottoms was cracking and spitting like a long fuse ready to detonate an explosion. The various fingers of fire were reaching for the drainage down to the creek and then dying in the wet bottoms. There was no reason in the fire. It would run with the wind, turning at one point and going a different direction. As the fire turned toward the rocky hills, it began to die out.

Zach and Bill's ranch buildings were spared but some of the ranchers lost their buildings and many of their cattle. The people who escaped the fire pitched in and helped the others. They housed many families until their buildings could be rebuilt. It was a community effort to help anyone that needed it.

The fire turned before it reached Zach and Bill's cattle, but they were very disturbed, and it took a long time and hard riding to get them back as a herd.

Barbed wire was introduced in the U.S. in 1874. Zach and Jim were busy stringing wire on some of his range. He felt he could control his herd and keep them together for easier feeding. When one area was grazed they would move the cattle to another fenced area. Zach bought a wire stretcher that worked like a pump. The men had to be careful while stringing the wire as one slip would hurt a man very badly, around the neck or legs or even cut a man's hand off.

By 1876, the cattle industry was recovering from the panic of three years before and there was a steady demand for cattle. From 1876 to 1880, the cattle business expanded on a steady or rising market.

1876 was a big year as it was the year Colorado was admitted to the Union as a state. Cattle prices rose again and everyone was making a profit. In June of that year, the Battle of the "Little Big Horn" was fought. General Custer and 253 of his men were killed. Only forty-two Indians lost their lives. This event caused continued worry among the ranchers. The Indians did not travel south but stayed in the Dakotas and Wyoming.

As the years went by, the ranchers were still finding success from their endeavor. They did have a little trouble with the Indians from time to time. The sheriff called a meeting in the Grange Hall asking for volunteers to act as scouts in the area between Lamar and Eads, looking for renegades. Zach felt he should do his duty, so he volunteered for a two week stretch.

He knew that Jim could handle the ranch alone as he was now a man and was very capable.

Mandy was upset with his decision because she was still very frightened of the Indians. When the men were scouting, they found several Indians camped along the rivers. They would ride to the nearby Fort and report. The soldiers would drive them back to their reservation.

The trouble continued for several years. Little wars would spring up in all territories, mostly north of Chivington in Wyoming and the Dakotas. The unrest worried the ranchers, but all they could do was hope the trouble would stay in the plains. Zach, Mandy, and the boys were well settled on their ranch.

Mark was now ten years old with his own horse and rode to school each day. He felt so grown up as his father let him go with some of the cowboys when they were on a short circle.

Babe was eight and had his own horse. He rode to school with Mark. He was a small boy so couldn't ride the range with Mark until he was stronger. He helped his mother in the garden, fed the chickens, and gathered the eggs.

Life was good this year after so many bad ones.

CHAPTER FORTY-ONE

OVER THE YEARS

In 1877, Mandy and Zach were blessed with a little girl born in February, they named her Bess. They were so happy to have a girl. The boys were very excited having a sister to make over and love.

The winter of 1877 was a hard one. It had stopped raining for months at a time. They heard the fury of the winter wind as it came whining across the short burned grass. It cut the flesh when they were out riding.

They strained their eyes, watching through the long summer day for the rain that never came. They tossed through hot nights, with worry, and rose only to find the worst nightmares, the cattle grazing on the brown stubble.

Another disaster, plagues of grasshoppers were even more devastating than the heat and drought. They descended on the ranches in great clouds that blotted out the sun and quickly devoured every green, living thing, the young grain, the vegetable gardens even the trees along the creek. They covered the walls of the houses and sometimes worked their way indoors to feast on the curtains. Absolutely nothing could be done until they moved on to another location. Railroads were forced to hire men to shovel the pests off the tracks. With the engine's wheels running over endless grasshoppers, the rails became so slippery that no traction could be obtained.

In spite of all such difficulties and hardship, the ranchers survived the bad years and clung tenaciously to their new land. There was always the strong faith that their luck would change, conditions improve, and the next year bring a fine harvest.

Come fall the winter snows started early. This brought hope the moisture would return again. Several inches of snow fell during the long winter. It seemed normal weather had at last returned, snows, wind, thaws, and refreezes. Zach had stored enough feed to carry them through the long months.

They were surprised the way the grass grew back with the spring rains. It was the first measurable rain they had for many months. With the greening of the valleys, it was so beautiful looking toward the house snugged up against the northern lip of the valley. The fenced hay meadow in the bottoms to the grasses that rose gently to the ranch buildings. The whitewashed barn with the great hayloft and the stout corral made of poles brought down from the mountains. Zach left the house its natural brown color. Maybe someday he would paint it but not for now.

Much to the surprise of Mandy and Zach, another girl arrived in March of 1879. They named her Mary. The boys were really taken back, now two girls.

Cattle began to rise in price in 1878 and 79. Range stock sold at $7.00 or $8.00 a head by the herd range delivery. By the end of 1880, the price was about $9.50 and by the end of 1881, it was $12.00. Range cattle were selling from $30.00 to $35.00 per head in 1882 when the boom was at its height.

In 1884, the drought was severe. Cattlemen divided into two camps. Free grass men used wire cutters and cut the fences. Future ranchmen would have to operate under a system of fenced pastures if he had purchased no open range.

The scrub stock and longhorn had to be replaced with a better grade of beef cattle. The blooded Hereford bull would cost from $100.00 to $500.00. The bull must be protected, sheltered, and fed, if necessary, for the investment to be saved and the herd improved. Zach was happy to have acquired his bull early on before the prices were too high. His bull was getting older, and he had to make plans to find another one. With careful shopping he was able to find a good one at one of the auctions. He also found several head of cattle to add to his herd. He felt he had his ranch in good shape for the years to come and would not have to make any more large purchases.

CHAPTER FORTY-TWO

ZACH'S GROWING FAMILY

Life on the Bar Z continued with good times and bad times. All in all Zach's and Mandy's ranch was considered one of the top ranches in Southeastern Colorado.

Things were very different with the arrival of two more children. The girls kept Mandy busy. She was busy making dresses and blankets for the girls. The boys couldn't wait to get home from school to see their little sisters.

She had her hands full now with two babies, and she still had to cook for the family. So it was decided that the boys had to take over the duties outside the house. They took charge of the chickens and come spring they had to plant and take care of the garden, with Mandy looking over their efforts.

Zach was a happy man with two boys and now two girls. He felt they now had a perfect family. Life continued, working the ranch, going to church on Sunday and attending Saturday night meetings at the Grange once a month.

In the fall of 1880, Mark moved to Lamar so that he could attend boarding school. Chivington did not have a high school program for the children, and he wanted to have a high school diploma so he could go on and become a surveyor. At an early age, he spent a lot of time with the fellows that worked on the railroad. He decided he wanted to follow this type of work because he felt it was a better way to make a living. Ranching was hard work and he didn't like the long hours.

Zach was disappointed because he hoped his boys would take

over the ranch in the future. Mark left the ranch at the age of 17 and went to Denver to continue his studies. After Mark left Babe, now 15, took over the work Mark had been doing.

About this time the City Council decided a school had to be built. So many people had moved into the territory with their children, they needed more space. Miss Snyder had been teaching in the Grange Hall as she didn't have room in her house for all of the children.

It was decided to build a two room school so the older children would have a more detailed education. That meant another teacher had to be found. At the same time Miss Snyder announced she was going to be married at Christmas time.

The search was on for two teachers. Luck was with them as they found a husband and wife, both certified as teachers and were willing to take over the job. George and Nancy Fleming moved from Kansas City to Lamar a short time ago and were happy to have a chance to work together in their chosen field.

This proved to be a good move as they could have a high school program for all the children that wanted to further their education.

The wedding of Miss Snyder was a grand affair. She had taught the children of Chivington and the surrounding ranches for many years, was well loved by all, and was going to be missed. She married a railroad supervisor who had been working in the area for few years and was now being transferred to Eads.

It was now 1883, and Mandy presented Zach with another girl in January. They called her Gracie. She was a beautiful child, blond curly hair like her mother's and big blue eyes. The girls were so happy with the new baby. Mark was away at school and Babe was too busy with all the ranch work, he didn't have much time for the girls.

Zach arranged to have one of the men to help Babe with the chickens and garden as Mandy had to spend all of her time taking care of the house and girls.

Babe finished high school but didn't feel the need for any additional education. He stayed on the ranch helping Zach. As the years went by they had their ups and downs true to life on the range. The older girls went to school, as the boys did, on horse back.

On a hot summer day in 1889, the girls were playing in the yard. Gracie, now six years old, let out a scream. Mandy came running to find a large rattlesnake curled up near Gracie.

Without a thought of the danger she grabbed the child and ran with her into the house, yelling to the children to get their Papa from the barn.

Zach rode to town for Dr. Ben while Mandy looked for the bite. She knew what to do. She cut the leg just above the knee and tried to draw the poison out. By the time Zach and Dr. Ben got back to the ranch, the small child had died. Gracie was only six years old. The family and all of their friends felt the grief deeply. The whole family grieved for years to come as little Gracie was the center of all of their lives.

In the fall of 1890, still another baby girl arrived. She was named Lucy. Mandy had delivered six children, four girls and two boys. With the loss of Gracie, there were now only five.

Mark came home for a visit every few months, only to go on to another adventure. He traveled to Texas and liked it so much he decided to stay. It was years before he came to visit again. Mandy missed her oldest so very much, but she knew that he had to be on his own.

Babe, at the age of 22 decided he didn't want the ranch life either. He moved to Oregon with some of his friends. He settled in the northern part of the state near the Columbia River.

Zach continued with the ranch with the help of hired hands. Jim was now his foreman and was responsible for running the ranch. Jim never married as he dreamed about in his early years.

CHAPTER FORTY-THREE

THE GIRLS GET MARRIED

Bess was the first of the girls to marry. She was only sixteen. She met a fellow while attending many of the Saturday nights at the Grange. He had quite a way with the girls and took a liking to Bess at once. In his mind, he thought she would be a good catch as her father was such a successful rancher.

He said he had a big ranch north of Chivington. No one had seen his place, but he sure put on a good show. He even fooled Mandy and Zach. They liked him for what he appeared to be. They were married in 1893.

After several months, Mandy and Zach became concerned about Bess. Mack, her husband showed up in Chivington from time to time, spending most of his time in the saloon and card room. Zach ran into him one day and asked about Bess. He said she didn't want to come to town, wanted to stay at home. That didn't seem right as Bess always liked to shop and visit with her friends.

Early one morning, Zach hitched the horses to the wagon to pay a visit. When he got to Mack's ranch, he was shocked. Only a mud house with no floor and half of the windows were boarded up because the glass had been broken. Bess was in bad shape. She was so thin and white. No color to her cheeks and her hair hung in a long straggly mass.

Zach decided he was going to take her home. She said she couldn't go because she was married to the man and had to stay. He wouldn't listen to her. She and her things were packed in the wagon, and they headed back to the Bar Z.

When Mack got home and found her gone, his first thought was someone had kidnapped her. When he found her things were gone, he wondered how she could get away. What to do next? He spent the night wondering how she got away. He decided he had better tell her folks, so he rode over to Zach's ranch. As he rode up to the entrance of the ranch, he was stopped by the hired hands. They told him he wasn't welcome and to be on his way. Zach and Bess were leaving for Lamar at once to have the marriage canceled. He protested. She was his wife and would remain so. About that time, Zach rode up with his shotgun and told him to get. Mack knew he couldn't fight Zach's wishes, as by now Zach knew the shape of things at his place.

Zach put Bess up in the hotel in Lamar and told her to stay and recover from this sad experience. She was glad to do so as she was so ashamed. Divorce was not the thing to do. When married, you were to stay married forever. How was she ever going to look at her friends and family again?

After a few weeks, Zach brought Bess back home. Her family gathered around her and told her the error in judgement was as much theirs as it was hers. They should have checked this man out before the marriage. Bess decided she would go to Pueblo and get her teaching certificate. Within a year, she was certified and started teaching in Pueblo. She couldn't come home for a visit until the following spring.

Bess taught for several years. She decided she was better off as a single woman. She had admired Miss Snyder so much she thought it would be nice to follow in her footsteps.

One spring Bess came home for a visit and told her family that she and another teacher were going to St. Louis for the fair. This shocked Zach and Mandy because women should not travel without an escort. She said she thought they were old enough. This was 1904 and times have changed and women traveled alone all the time.

While they were at the fair Bess met this fine gentleman. He was a widower with three boys. His wife had passed away over a year ago. Bess asked him to come to Colorado to meet her family. She didn't want to make another mistake in a marriage and wanted their approval before deciding what she should do. They took a liking to Wes as soon as they met.

Zach wanted to be sure. He suggested he would go back to Missouri with him to meet the boys and the rest of the family. Wes was happy to have Zach come, and he wanted Bess to come also to meet the family. Wes had a good job with the government and had been with them for several years.

The wedding date was set and Mandy, Zach, and Lucy made the trip for the wedding in the spring of 1905.

Wes's boys were fine, but still remembered their mother and accepted Bess as only their father's wife, not as a new mother. This made it hard for Bess because she wanted to make a complete family.

Zach, Mandy, and Lucy came home to the Bar Z. They all thought this would be a fine marriage. In the spring of 1907, they got a letter from Bess telling them she was pregnant and was sick most of the time. She planned delivering in July and asked Mandy if she would come and be with her.

She sounded so frightened, Zach and Mandy planned to go and be with her for the delivery. Bess had a hard time with the birth. She lived only a few hours after the baby arrived. Wes was broken with his and their loss. Here was a beautiful baby boy with no mother. What was he to do?

Mandy said to him, "We'll take him home with us and you can come anytime to see him. After all, he is your son."

So it was done—another baby in the house. Mandy was beginning to feel she was getting too old to raise another baby. Lucy came to the rescue and gave up riding with the men and stayed in the house to care for baby Marc. Wes named him after Bess' brother Mark.

Lucy was the only one left at home. She was very active and loved riding the range with the men, and had been riding from the age of 10. Mandy didn't like the idea of a girl riding with the men, but she couldn't convince her it was not the thing to do. Lucy had a host of gentlemen callers, but she wouldn't give any of them a second thought. She just loved ranching and being outdoors in all kinds of weather.

As time went by, Wes made many trips to visit his son. Lucy thought he was such a fine man, and he loved his son so.

While Bess was having her problems, life went on for Mary. She had met a fine gentleman named Charles. He was stationed in Chivington as a railroad supervisor for the area. They were married in 1897. After a few years he was transferred to Cheyenne Wells, a little town west and north of Chivington. This was a fine marriage producing four children.

Three years went by and Wes asked Lucy to be his wife. Lucy was such a strong and headstrong person, everyone was surprised she said yes.

In August of 1910, Lucy married Wes and they moved to Missouri taking Marc with them. Lucy, being of strong mind, got the boys whipped into shape in no time. There was no question who was in charge of the home. The boys were much older now so they were not home much after they were married.

Lucy and Wes were married 10 years before she delivered a little girl, the only child of this union.

With the children all gone, Zach and Mandy were feeling time catching up with them. Zach was now in his sixties.

They decided they would have to sell the ranch. Zach could no longer make the long rides and pitch the hay. When the deal was made they moved to a small town north of Denver, Colorado.

Zach died in 1922 and Mandy followed him in 1929.